his
pirate

Love on the High Seas

seductress

his pirate

Love on the High Seas

seductress

TAMARA HUGHES

Entangled Publishing, LLC
2614 South Timberline Road
Suite 109
Fort Collins, CO 80525
Visit our website at www.entangledpublishing.com.

Scandalous is an imprint of Entangled Publishing, LLC.

Edited by Erin Molta
Cover Design by Louisa Maggio
Cover Art by iStock

ISBN 978-1-68281-057-6

Manufactured in the United States of America

First Edition November 2015

To Ron and Shirley Bores. You've been such a great support to me. I truly appreciate all that you've done.

Chapter One

November 1724

Bloody pirates!

The mizzenmast at his back, Thomas Glanville, captain of the *Argo Navis*, the finest vessel in Lamont Shipping's fleet, slashed his sword at the two pirates who attacked him. He'd hoped he was done fighting pirates after his adventure as first mate to James Lamont. Unfortunately not. And yet, not a twinge of fear invaded his heart. In fact, in a sick sort of way, he enjoyed the challenge, the test of his skill. If it weren't for the lives of his crew and the fate of his ship, he might toy with these vultures a bit longer. Instead, he sliced one across the middle and the other across the throat. They both fell to the decking, their pitiful lives cut short.

Through the haze of smoke from cannon fire, he surveyed the battle waging around him. Sweet mother in heaven. The ship had sustained more damage than he'd thought. The torn foresail hung clear to the decking, and the mainmast had cracked. Outmanned and still recovering from the illness that had plagued the crew these last two days, his men were losing the struggle. He raced down the stairs to the main deck and his first mate. Although Hugh was holding his own, his face was pale and his movements were weak.

Stepping past the wounded and dead, Thomas came up from behind and dispatched the devil who had Hugh bleeding from cuts on his leg and shoulder.

"Are you well?" Thomas asked Hugh.

Hugh nodded, then crumpled to the planks, his eyes rolling back in his head.

No time to help him. Another pirate attacked, this one dealing a decisive strike toward Thomas's ribs. With a quick move, he evaded the swing and assessed his opponent. The pirate held a saber in his right hand and a dagger in his left, which meant the bounder would likely block with his sword and strike out with the shorter blade.

Thomas dodged another swing and thrust forward, only to be deflected. The pirate had a small build. Using brute strength, Thomas should be able to overpower…her? Thomas's gaze caught on the pirate's face, a face with soft, feminine features. *What in heaven's name?* She struck again. This time, his sidestep wasn't quite quick enough, and her blade scored his outer thigh. The resulting sting restored him to his senses. "*You're* a pirate?" Obviously. Still, hard to believe. He pressed forward, forcing on her a series of blows meant to test her strength and will.

She parried and blocked his every move with an aptitude that amazed. "Aye. A pirate, *and* captain of the *Sea Sprite*," she boasted, a wry smile upon her full lips.

Indeed, she appeared very much a pirate in her men's garb—a threadbare, brown suit with overly long sleeves she'd had to roll up. Her ebony hair had been pulled back in a queue and was half hidden beneath a rumpled tricorn. Also, like her men, was her look of desperation and the grim cast to her countenance that bespoke of a hard existence.

"We offered you quarter," she said as she evaded his thrust with ease. "Why didn't you surrender? You had to know we outnumbered you."

He didn't answer. In all honesty, he'd thought they could defeat the pirates, if not with cannon fire, then with skill. After hearing of all the pirate attacks of late, they'd hired on additional hands, men who could fight. If it hadn't been for the damn illness…

"It's not too late. You can save what's left of your crew. Surrender now, Captain Glanville, and we'll see that your men are ransomed back." A wicked gleam brightened her eyes as if victory would soon be hers.

He should do as she asked. It would be the sensible thing, but pride kept him from saying the words. Not yet. He still had another opponent to defeat, and so far she hadn't been an easy one to overcome. Despite his steady attack, she kept her muscles relaxed, her balance sure. Her attention followed his movements no matter how small, adjusting her stance, looking for weaknesses. "How do you know I'm Captain Glanville?" When work was at hand, he didn't dress any differently than his men.

"I know much about you." Stepping clear of two men battling to their left, she blocked his sword with her own and lunged with her dagger. He jumped from the blade, avoiding injury by the barest inch. This one relied on speed and accuracy rather than power. Smart woman.

"What do you want from us?" he asked, launching an attack of his own, this time with so much force and speed, she had no choice but to retreat until her back came up against the railing. "We only just left London four days ago. Our cargo is mainly iron and ale."

Her gaze sharpened even as her expression became strained. His assault was wearing her down. "I want the Ruby Cross."

How the hell did she know he had the cross? And did she believe he'd simply hand it over? Hand over a priceless antiquity of the Knights Templar? Absurd. He swung his sword all the harder. The clang of steel rang through the air. Her reactions slowed, and her arms trembled. He made a final cut, putting all his strength behind the blow, and knocked her sword from her hand. Triumph surged through his veins. She attempted to slash out with her dagger. He grabbed her arm before her blade could reach him and hauled her close, their faces nose to nose. "You'll never take the cross from me," he vowed as he towered over her, his grip strong.

The point of a sword touched his back. Thomas tensed, and he swore beneath his breath, self-disgust heavy in his chest. The distraction of this one woman had sealed his fate.

Bloody hell.

· · ·

Catherine's cheeks flamed. Struggling to catch her breath, she stood mere inches from Captain Thomas Glanville, his grasp on her firm. The air tasted of smoke and ash, and her sword-wielding arm ached to high heaven. This close, she could feel the heat from Glanville's body warm the chilly November air. Even with a sword to his back, his green eyes smoldered with defiance.

Blast. He would have won if not for Barnet's sword poking into his spine.

Yanking her arm from Glanville's hold, she stared him straight in the eye. "You're wrong. The Ruby Cross will be mine."

She sheathed her dagger. *Sorry, dear brother.* Emmett would be sorely disappointed after all the hours he'd spent teaching her how to wield her saber. Although, in her defense, her brother's sparring hadn't adequately prepared her for Glanville, a man who fought with such ferocity. Obviously, he was a well-seasoned combatant. Which might explain the slight crook to his nose.

Two men grasped Glanville's arms and jerked him away from her, and Barnet, the *Sea Sprite's* quartermaster, lowered his sword. "Ah, Catherine. You should have listened and stayed aboard the *Sea Sprite,*" Barnet scolded, the scar on his upper lip stretching with his frown.

Glanville watched her with interest.

"Be silent, Barnet," she hissed, surveying her crew for any sign of antipathy. "I'll not listen to your nonsense." Detecting no mockery or derision from the men, she cast her quartermaster a glare. *Damn, Barnet, chastising me in front of the men. I am the captain here. Stay aboard the Sea Sprite, indeed.* She could hold her own with a sword…or so she'd thought. Catherine directed her attention back to Glanville, the rest of the merchantman's crew subdued. She'd deal with Barnet later. "Where is the cross?" she demanded.

Glanville's blond head bowed, and he studied the deck for the briefest of moments before those green eyes came to rest on her again. "It's not on board."

"You're lying." She'd seen enough charlatans on the streets of St. Giles to know. And Glanville had all the makings of a crook. Calm when faced with danger, his movements controlled…a cocksure devil if she ever saw one. "Search the ship," she called out to those of her crew not busy with captives, although the likelihood they would find the cross wasn't good. To her knowledge, both this ship and Glanville's house had been searched by Simon Brewer's men. Her heart quickened its pace, and a shiver raced over her skin. Just the thought of that vile man holding her mother and son for ransom, for a treasure only Captain Thomas Glanville could provide… Clenching her teeth, she retrieved her sword and approached Glanville, drawing her dagger once more. She set the blade to his throat. "Where have you hidden the Ruby Cross?"

He shrugged, a bare shift of shoulders given the grip the men had on him. "I already told you. It's not here."

"Tell me where it is, then," she bit out. She needed that cross. Her son's life depended on it.

Infuriatingly dispassionate, his reaction was to raise his chin, exposing more of his throat. "Kill me, and you'll never get answers."

He was right, of course. Torture would be needed. The thought sickened her, but she kept her expression grim and her voice firm. "I don't intend to kill you…at least not yet." She shifted her blade, enough to add more venom to her words, and envisioned cutting his skin. But the stench of blood from the dead and injured around them filled her nostrils, and the groans of the wounded ate at her nerves.

Crew members of the *Sea Sprite* returned one by one, each empty-handed. Not a surprise. And yet, an edge of panic tensed her shoulders. *What if they never find the cross? What if...?* Stop. She couldn't think that way. Too much was at stake. Still, the hand holding her dagger trembled. "If you wish to save your men and yourself, speak up."

Glanville narrowed his eyes, a stubborn set to his chin. "Do what you must. I'll never tell you what you want to know."

"Allow me, Cap'n." Barnet stepped forward with a menacing glower and a knife in hand.

"No. Stand down." The crew had elected her as captain for this voyage out of deference to her late husband Peter, the true captain of the *Sea Sprite*. A mixture of grief and anger throbbed within her chest. Peter, the scoundrel, had left her and their son six years ago on a quest for riches, only to die as poor as he'd always been. Nevertheless, if she wanted the crew's respect, she'd best handle this situation herself.

Barnet lowered his weapon and stepped aside, although he looked none too happy. "As you wish, Cap'n."

She scanned the decks, desperation flaring bright. "If not you, Glanville, then perhaps your men will suffer," she taunted as her stomach churned, the smell of death and gore taking their toll.

Her captive nodded toward a man sprawled unconscious on the deck whose face was deathly pale. "There's my first mate. You're welcome to torture him. I don't think he'll mind."

She scowled and ran her blade's edge over the skin at his

throat. The thin line bloomed red. "No, I think I'll test your mettle first. A few scars might improve your looks." Her voice didn't waver, even as bile rose in her throat. Although she had spilled blood during the battle, torturing a man was an entirely different skill, one she had yet to master. And she would. Later. At this moment, if she had to cut this man until he howled in pain, her sparse luncheon would make a reappearance on her boots. The last thing she needed was to vomit before her crew.

Despite her roiling gut, she braced her feet apart and addressed her men with authority. "We have no time to waste. Take the prisoners below and lock them away. We'll split our numbers between the two ships and head back to London." She nodded toward Glanville. "This one will be strung up in his cabin. Never fear. By the time we reach port, I'll have the cross in my hand." She would do whatever she had to, even make this man's life a living hell if it were required, and judging by the arrogance of Thomas Glanville, that possibility was quite likely.

Chapter Two

Catherine watched as Glanville was tied with rope to the wall in his large captain's cabin, his arms secured over his head. He didn't fight his bondage. Instead, his piercing gaze never left her. Perhaps he was reserving his strength—a wise move. Not that it would matter. He *would* tell her where the cross was hidden. She'd see to that.

After the ropes were tied tight, the men pulled the boots from his fcct and began to scavenge his pockets.

"Go," she commanded. "This one is mine."

Their search for valuables stopped, although one man picked up the boots as he headed out. Very well. She had no use for them, anyway.

"Close the door," she ordered as her men left. She didn't need an audience. She'd never tortured a man, and it might take a few goes before she got the hang of it. Her pulse skipped a beat at the thought, her nerves twitchy. The door shut, she set aside all doubt and approached her prisoner.

"Shall we begin?"

A smirk lifted a corner of his lips. "Whenever you're ready, *my lady*."

So smug and confident. How annoying. She unsheathed her dagger and settled it along his ear. He didn't need two of them, did he? He'd be fine with just one. She squelched any weak thoughts that sprang forward. She'd be strong, for her son.

Those green eyes mocked her, and his arse leaned into her blade as if daring her to slice him, nicking himself in the process. A single drop of blood oozed from the cut on his cheek. And damn it if her softer instincts didn't rise at the sight. She wanted to blot the wound with a clean cloth and sooth the ache with comforting words, just as she would with family or friends.

Family, like her mother and son. *Oh God. Jonas.* Was he hurt? Or ill? And her mother. She was already a sickly woman, ever tired and weak. Would she survive Simon Brewer's imprisonment?

Her resolve strengthened. "Listen here. I will hurt you, if I must."

"No, you won't. You don't have it in you."

She stared at his slightly crooked nose, and those green eyes that dared and defied, a frown on her face. "You don't know what I'm capable of." She would do anything for her family.

His brows slanted, and a serious look infused his features. "If you truly intended to cause me pain, you'd have done the deed on deck, or let your quartermaster do the job."

Catherine lowered her blade. He was right. The mere thought of drawing his blood churned her stomach, and it didn't matter whether the deed was done by her hand or not. As much as she needed the cross, she couldn't obtain it by that means. But there were other ways. "We'll see how you fare without food and water."

A chuckle laced his breath. "That method of persuasion will take some time."

"I'm a patient woman," she lied, her mind already grasping for other ideas with which to provide quicker results. Would reasoning work? "Why do you want the cross? You're the captain of this ship, not its owner. All cargo belongs to your employer, Gordon Lamont."

"He has nothing to do with the cross. *I* made the arrangements to obtain it, and *I'll* arrange its sale."

"And with the profits…?"

He paused, his gaze settling on her. "I'll buy my own ship."

Ambition and pride. Her husband had been driven by the same need. In fact, his ambition had become more important to him than his wife and son. Nothing should come between a man and his family. Nothing. "What if I told you I need the Ruby Cross to save two people I care for very much? Family."

"You're lying. You'd say anything to get what you want."

"But I speak the truth. My son Jonas is seven years old, and my mother…"

His expression, ripe with stubborn cynicism, stopped her from saying more. He didn't believe her. Just as she'd expected. She had seized his ship and taken his crew hostage, after all. In his mind, she'd say anything to get the cross, and in that much, he was right. Just the same, she was learning what sort of man Glanville was. She scanned the room. "I don't believe you would leave the cross in the care of someone else. Not if obtaining and selling it is *your* responsibility." She glanced at him, but he remained still and silent. No mocking. No denials. Encouraging.

Catherine moved around the immense cabin that took up the width of the ship, keeping Glanville in her sight. "No, you would want to keep it close at hand." No matter where she paused, he didn't so much as twitch. Damn. He would make a good card player. Ah, hell. What would it hurt? She opened the armoire and rifled through his belongings. Next, the table by the bed, a chest in the corner, his desk, and finally the bed itself. Was the cross hidden in the mattress? She almost tore the thing apart in her quest. Nothing.

When she turned back to her captive, he was smiling arrogantly. The lout. "It has to be here," she grumbled. And yet, for all she knew, he could have it on his person right now. She looked him over, from his black breeches to his long-sleeved white shirt, left open to reveal a smattering of blond hair on his chest. From what Brewer had told her, the Ruby Cross should be roughly the length of her hand, made of gold and covered in rubies, the center stone the size of a Spanish doubloon. No, Glanville didn't have it on his person.

"You'll never find the cross," he insisted, quite pleased with himself.

Aha. "So you admit it's on this ship, perhaps in this very room."

His smile broadened. "If you let me go, we might come to an agreement."

What a cocky, irritating… "Do you believe me a fool?"

He didn't answer. He didn't need to. So far he'd outwitted her at every turn. Maybe if she had cut off his ear, she'd have the cross already. If only she could bring him low in a different way. Hurt his precious pride. She pulled her dagger from her belt.

"Will you attempt to cut me again?"

She yanked the tails of his white shirt from his breeches, and his eyes widened for an instant.

"What are you planning?"

Catherine bristled at the amusement in his voice. He could laugh all he wanted when he stood tied to a wall utterly naked. A little humiliation might do him good.

She sliced through the material of his shirt, first up the front, then down each sleeve. Pulling the fabric from him and dropping it to the floor, she studied his well-muscled chest, sculptured curves, and smooth skin. The sight dried her throat, and she had to swallow to regain some moisture. She hadn't seen a man's bare chest in ages, and this one was by far the most tempting she'd seen in her life. She itched to reach out and slide her hand over the wide expanse. The mere thought tickled deep in her belly.

She peered into his face, and sharp eyes glared back, all humor gone, replaced by annoyance. Good. Now he might take her seriously. "Where has your wit gone?" she taunted.

Their stares locked, she removed his belt and freed the buttons of his breeches as a muscle tensed in his jaw. She felt a bulge in his pocket, and investigated the source. A silver pocket watch, on its lid an intricate painting of a ship at sea. Exquisite, and undoubtedly very valuable. Glanville pinned her with a look of pure fury. The watch must be significant to him. She slipped the piece into her pocket, to be used later as needed.

Catherine lowered her knife to his waist. Glanville's

dark gaze watched her every move. The top of his breeches open, she slid her blade between his skin and the fabric. He shivered and his hips drew back the barest inch. "Don't move," she chided, satisfaction bringing a smile to her lips.

He growled in response, the sound low and guttural, and bumps rose along her flesh. She cut the material away in an easy stroke from waist to knee, then completed the task on his other leg. He drew in a shaky breath as she tugged the shredded breeches from his body. His lower half was as magnificent as the rest of him. Strong, muscular thighs and an impressive erection that made her insides pool with warmth. Dear Lord. Was she torturing this man or herself? Blushing, she quickly removed his hose, and stepped away to steady her pulse.

His humiliation complete—and hers as well—she demanded, "Tell me what I want to know."

A cocksure smile tugged at his lips again. "Or what? You'll pleasure me?"

Her fists clenched so hard, her fingernails dug into her palms, and she uttered a curse so foul, her mother would have had cause to issue a lecture. As she should, after all the time she'd spent teaching Catherine to speak like a woman highborn.

Glanville laughed. "Such a lady... Which begs the question, how is it that when you're not cursing, you usually speak in the vernacular of a proper lady, even as you stand before me, the captain of a ship full of pirates?"

Good question. Why her mother had gone to such lengths was beyond her. Her mother had been naught but a lady's maid. And Catherine, she would never climb out of the London squalor, no matter her diction or dialect.

"I should shave your head." Maybe that would take him down a peg or two.

"Do it," he chuckled. "I have no vanity. In fact, I've always wondered what I'd look like without hair." He turned his head to the side to give her a better view. "I believe I have a rather well-shaped head. Don't you agree?"

Oh! Before she could mutter an oath even more vulgar than the last, she stormed from the cabin, slammed the door shut behind her, and marched across the deck. Thomas Glanville would be the end of her sanity. He had no shame, no humility—

"How goes it?"

Her heart nearly jumped from her chest. So consumed with disparaging her captive's name, she almost ran into Barnet, who'd apparently been lurking close by.

She released a long exhale. "Not as well as I'd like," she admitted, then remembered. "I need to talk to you."

Barnet settled his hands on her shoulders, a compassionate look softening his face. "Speak freely. What is it?"

She pulled his hands away. This was exactly the kind of behavior her men shouldn't be seeing. Barnet treating her as a friend, rather than his captain. "You can't be chiding me in front of the crew."

"When did I…?"

"Telling me I should have stayed on the *Sea Sprite* to avoid the battle." She shook her head. "I can't have the crew thinking I'm weak."

"Beggin' your forgiveness, Catherine. I don't want to see you injured, is all. We've been friends a long time, aye?"

"Aye, we have." She took in Barnet's haggard features and his threadbare clothes. He'd been through tough times of late. They both had. "I appreciate your concern, but if I'm to be captain this voyage, you can't be questioning my decisions."

"I see. Well then, if I can't help you in that way, at least I can do somethin' about Glanville." Barnet walked toward the cabin door, determination in his stride, already pulling his knife from its sheath.

"No! Wait!" She hurried after him and grabbed his arm before he'd gone too far. What would he think when he saw Glanville—naked and uninjured?

Barnet turned to face her with a questioning look. "Not to worry. I wager I'll have your cross by the end of the day. Leave Glanville to me. I'll start with a few cuts with me blade, then a simple floggin', and if that don't work, I'll have him hung by his genitals while I feed him his own nose."

Jesus, Joseph, and Mary! She'd never get that horrid image out of her head. "Your services won't be necessary, Wolfrie," she hurried to assure him.

He cast her an ill-tempered look. Oh, yes. "Sorry." He'd never liked his given name.

"As for Glanville, this is something *I* need to do. But I'll think on your suggestions. Might even use one of them." Or not.

He nodded once. "If it's what you be wantin'."

"It is." Thomas Glanville might be arrogant and irritating as hell, but he was an innocent man in all this. She wouldn't allow him to be abused in such a way. Instead, she would wait for hunger and thirst to coax him into compliance. Or perhaps ply him with alcohol. Whatever she chose, she would get him to talk, but she would do it her own way.

. . .

His shoulders aching and the cool evening air chilling him, Thomas watched Catherine enter the cabin bearing a platter of food and a bottle of rum. "Hungry?" she asked. The wench. She wouldn't give him any food. Of that he was sure. His stomach growled at the heady smell of mutton. She'd also brought cheese and a loaf of bread. His mouth watered.

She set her burden on the table and stabbed a piece of meat with a fork. With a confident smile, she stepped closer, waving the food just beyond his nose. "Would you like a bite?"

He did his best to disregard the offering, closing his eyes against the sight. If only he could shut out the tantalizing scent as well.

"You can have all you want…if you reveal the location of the cross."

Thomas held his silence but stared her in the eye just to prove himself steadfast. Food, or the lack thereof, wouldn't sway him. Hell, a day had yet to pass. If he succumbed after one day, he was a weak sot indeed.

"A pity. Still, best not let it go to waste." She popped the morsel into her mouth and chewed, her gaze lifting heavenward. "*Mmm.* Delicious."

He didn't falter, and she turned away, but not before he spied the frustration that tensed her features. By the time she returned to the table and faced him, the look was gone. "Your men eat and drink well. My crew isn't used to such luxuries." She gestured toward the door, through which laughter and shouts could be heard.

"No need to keep me company. Go celebrate with them." *And take the food with you.*

"Fraternize with the men?" She cocked her head to the side. "I'd much rather spend my time here with you."

Somehow he wasn't surprised by her choice. She hardly seemed the type to associate with pirates. What's more, she wasn't ruthless enough to captain a pirate crew. Barnet, on the other hand… "How did you come to be captain of that lot?"

"Rum?" she suggested, pouring a dram into a cup.

"Is it a sordid tale?" he teased. "Did you challenge and kill their former captain in a duel to the death?"

A frown darkened her comely face. "The prior captain was my husband."

"You didn't kill him then?" he mocked.

"He died in a sword fight, but not by my hand." She returned to his side, her expression grim. "Drink some rum," she ordered, lifting the cup to his lips.

He could refuse, but his parched throat begged otherwise. When she tilted the cup, he drank a swallow, welcoming its moisture and slightly sweet flavor. She kept the cup held high, and he finished the rest. More than he probably needed, but he wouldn't complain, particularly if it warmed him up a bit.

"More?" she asked as she filled the cup again.

Ah. "I see your ploy. Get me drunk to loosen my lips." *How clever.* Indeed, all her attempts to torment him so far had been soft. Unless she intended to make him talk out of sheer boredom. "I'll have more only if you join me."

She scowled, her beautiful brown eyes narrowing. "I could force you to drink," she snapped.

He laughed. So far she couldn't force him to do anything.

"Now why would you go to the trouble, when I'm offering to partake willingly?"

"How weary you make me," she grumbled, then pursed her lips as if she hadn't meant to admit that fact. She crossed the room to stand in front of him, bringing both the cup and bottle with her this time.

She raised the cup to his mouth, and he quirked a brow. "You first," he insisted.

After a long-suffering sigh, she relented, and took a sip, her nose wrinkling in distaste.

"Not much of a drinker?" He accepted the rum, and as expected, she had him finish the cup again. Good thing he could handle his liquor.

"Who has the time?" She flung her hand before him. "Those of us not born to wealth have to work endless hours to survive." Catherine poured another draught, and this time took a drink of her own accord. Apparently, the first sip hadn't been as distasteful as it had appeared.

He disregarded her comment about his wealth. Aye, he'd been born to a reasonably well-off existence, but that didn't mean he was a lazy bastard who relied on his family's money. "What work do you do?" he asked instead, after she'd poured more liquor down his throat.

Refilling the cup, she walked across the room and sat on the edge of his bed. "Anything," she cast him a pointed stare, "within reason." She took a sip of rum. "Sewing, washing, cooking, housework when an opening became available." Melancholy suffused her features. "I even worked for a butcher a long time ago."

Her struggle to survive wasn't unique. London was filled with similar tales of woe. And yet, the sorrow on her face touched a place inside him... Ah, hell. He shouldn't feel sorry for her. He stood here naked and tied to a wall. "Perhaps you shouldn't have married a pirate," he needled, pushing aside the pang of guilt once the words were out.

Her head snapped up, and her gaze ran him through. "I didn't marry a pirate. He became one long after we wed."

"And you didn't approve of his chosen profession." The bitterness in her voice said as much.

"He said he was going to better our circumstances. He said he would send home more coin than we'd ever had before." She drained the last drops from the glass and poured another draught. "No money ever came, and I never saw him again."

"He likely had nothing to send. I've come to understand that not all pirates are good at what they do." Like torturing prisoners. Although, in this case, he didn't mind.

She removed her tricorn and tossed it to the floor, then released her hair from its queue, shaking it out. Those dark tresses framed her face and settled over her shoulders in a riot of waves he couldn't help but admire. How soft would they be to the touch?

"It's not the money putting a burr in my bed."

What he wouldn't do to be that burr. Damn. Was it the rum putting such notions in his head?

She pointed her finger, at nothing in particular, wagging it as if she were speaking to her husband himself. "He left me to raise our son all on my own," she slurred slightly, "with no money to feed him or clothe him or..."

"Keep a roof over his head," he added when she couldn't seem to find the words.

"Yesss." She pulled off one of her boots, then the other,

revealing shapely calves concealed only by thin hose.

He tore his attention away, his throat dry for an entirely different reason than thirst. "Do you have no other family who can help you?"

Issuing a wide yawn, she shrugged. "My mother does what she can, although her health isn't what it used to be."

"What of your father? Or siblings?"

"My father, the butcher. When he lost his shop, he gave up all hope and ended his life rather than start over." She pulled back the bedcovers and unbuttoned her surcoat. "My brother did help us for a time, until he became a fugitive of the law. If he shows his face in London again, he'll surely hang."

"Who taught you to fight?" Someone had cared enough to train her to use a dagger and sword. And it must have taken some time, given her impressive skill.

"My brother. Emmett wanted me to be able to protect myself. Perhaps he knew someday I'd stand alone." Catherine shook her head. "It doesn't matter. I've learned I don't need no one…anyone…to get me through life." She doffed her worn coat, and Thomas could feel his blood drain to his groin. With a silent curse, he stared at her chest, where her shirt molded over her ample breasts, her nipples peaking. Sweet mercy.

"The only way to spare yourself disappointment from those around you…" she glanced his way and her eyes rounded, her gaze dropping to his engorged member before climbing back up to his face, "is to rely solely on yourself." She tossed the coat on the end of the bed and sauntered toward him, her breeches outlining slender legs and the apex between them.

She lifted the bottle in an absent gesture. "More rum?"

"I've —" He cleared his throat, but the tightness remained. "I've had enough."

"Very well," she purred, and the memory of her cutting off his clothing sprang to mind. His nudity had been of no consequence, but her touch and her burning looks had been true torture.

She closed the gap between them, her chest pressed against his in a way that inflamed his senses and made his manhood twitch. Rising on tiptoe, she whispered in his ear, "Do you like what you see?" Her rum-laced breath tickled his ear, sending a tremor down his spine.

He swallowed the moan that threatened, his body heating up like a well-stoked fire.

"Would you like to see more?" she asked, untying the opening of her shirt and pulling it aside to expose the alluring skin of her shoulder.

He couldn't put together a coherent thought. Not when he craved to nip and lick her shoulder and on to her graceful neck…her dainty ear…

She laid her hand on his chest and skimmed it over his skin, caressing him from his collarbone to his navel. He sucked in a long, wavering breath as her fingers glided over him, and his erection jerked again in anticipation that she might venture lower.

Glassy, brown eyes, dark as the finest ale, met his, her face so close, the tips of their noses almost touched. "Do you want to touch me…to kiss me?"

"Yes," he breathed. He'd like nothing better.

An inviting smile curved her mouth. "Tell me where you've hidden the cross and you can touch your lips to mine."

He tensed. *What a conniving vixen.* Before she had the sense to draw away, he pulled against his restraints, giving him enough leeway to capture her luscious lips with his own. He'd expected her to retreat, indignant or angry. Instead, she responded with a passion that jolted through him in a fiery wave of heat. She nestled closer, her tongue testing the seam of his lips. With a groan, he opened his mouth and let her explore at will. She tasted of sweet rum and warmth. How he longed to wrap his arms around her and hold her tight…to touch her everywhere. But he couldn't touch her at all, could he? A growl rumbled deep in his throat. Not while he was tied naked to a wall. He turned his head to the side, ending the kiss as abruptly as it had begun. Damn him for letting his lust overrule his better judgment.

She stumbled back a few steps, confusion followed by annoyance on her lovely face.

"What will you promise me next, Catherine? Can I touch your breasts if I give you a hint of the cross's location?"

Her features flushed, and she turned away, her balance slightly off as she walked to the bed. His bed. She removed her breeches and hose, providing a glimpse of thigh. He couldn't pull his gaze away from the view. Although her shirt hung to her knees, he admired her slender calves and tiny feet. She hurried into bed and drew the covers to her throat before blowing out the lantern and settling in.

Moonlight filtered through the wall of windows to his left, illuminating the room and the woman in the bed across from him. The fact that she'd been able to use his desires against him grated, and that he still burned for her… He ground his teeth. Accursed woman.

Her breathing soon became slow and even. He should

shout. Keep her awake, and dispense some torture of his own. Then again, what would stop her from moving to a different cabin to sleep blissfully in silence? No, he'd rather she stay here. For very close to where she lay, yes, almost by her head, the Ruby Cross was safely tucked away. The irony of it brought a smile to his face and an odd satisfaction to his heart.

Chapter Three

Her head aching, Catherine snuggled under the covers a bit more, but the morning sunlight burned through her lids straight into her skull. She ran her tongue over the roof of her mouth, wrinkling her nose at the awful taste. Burying her face in the pillow, she took refuge in the scent she found there. Manly. Like Thomas. Last evening's events came rushing back. The way she'd told him about her family and her troubles. She'd had no shame. And good Lord, that kiss. How wanton. She hadn't drunk that much rum, had she? She'd only meant to have enough to convince him to imbibe more, until he was truly drunk. Drunk enough to spill his secrets. She groaned. Instead, she'd been the one who'd done all the talking.

An icy chill infused the air, and she burrowed deeper under the blanket, sure she'd see her breath if she troubled herself to look. See her breath? Sweet heaven! She bolted up in bed and stared at Thomas. His head hung to his chest, and she could see him shiver clear across the room. She threw off the covers and sprang to her feet, the cold penetrating her shirt with its frigid claws. Her breath came out with a rush, and the air indeed clouded before her. When had the temperature dropped so low? While yesterday had been cooler than typical, she'd never imagined… Catherine rushed to his side. "Thomas?" Cupping his cheeks, she lifted his head. His eyes were closed and his lips blue. "Wake up!" She patted his face, then shook his shoulders, his skin so very cold.

With a moan and a wince, he opened his eyes. He glared at her as if only his hatred for her was keeping him from freezing to death.

"Don't worry. I'll fix this," she said as much to herself as to him. She raced to her pile of clothing and quickly donned her breeches. When she lifted her coat, the watch she'd taken from Thomas clattered to the floor. Without much thought, she set it on the table by the bed and hurried through the doorway. She pointed to two men loitering on deck. "You and you, I need your help. Follow me."

She led them into the cabin and motioned toward Thomas. "Move him to the bed."

They glanced between her and Thomas, breaking into grins.

"Just do as I say," she ordered.

They complied. Thomas moaned when his arms lowered to his sides, and he fell almost to the floor before they caught him. They half carried him to the bed and dropped him onto the mattress.

"Anything else, Cap'n?" one asked as they headed toward the door, snickering all the way.

Their impertinence rankled, but her concern right now was for Thomas. He appeared unconscious again. "Bring me some hot coffee, and be quick about—"

Barnet stood in the doorway, his stare sharp and angry.

"—it." Damn.

"What goes here?" Barnet demanded.

She hurried to Thomas's side and threw the covers over his nakedness. "He's suffering from the cold."

"Good." Barnet snatched the bedding and pulled it away from Thomas's shivering form. "Just what kind of torture are you performin' here?" He gestured toward her prisoner. "He's naked…with barely a scratch on him."

Heat rose up her neck and scalded her cheeks as she smacked Barnet's hands away and settled the covers over Thomas again. "Obviously what I'm doing is having some effect. Look at the condition he's in."

"And you're tendin' him like some nursemaid." He took her by the shoulders and moved her from the bed. "I don't think you understand the art of torture, Catherine. Now is the time to strike, when he's weak."

"He's not conscious." Even as she said the words, Thomas's eyes opened in narrow slits.

"A bucket of water would wake him."

Lifting her chin, she stood her ground. "No." She wouldn't let Thomas freeze to death, no matter how much she needed the cross. She wasn't going to let him die at all, and handing him over to Barnet would surely lead to his demise.

His features softening, Barnet lifted a lock of her hair and smoothed it between his fingers. "Torture isn't somethin' you should have to do—you've a tender heart. You should leave this work to me and my men."

She backed up a step and pulled her hair from his grasp. "What's gotten into you?" She'd always known he had softer feelings for her, but he'd never acted on them, and she encouraged nothing more than friendship. She had no interest in more from him. "And they're *my* men, not yours. Not on this voyage."

From the corner of her eye, she watched Thomas quirk a brow. "I am the captain, and I have this in hand," she assured Barnet.

Barnet's lips thinned and his jaw twitched, but he didn't lash out with that temper of his. Instead, he turned to Thomas, their glares clashing. Barnet grabbed one of Thomas's wrists and set to securing him to the bed. "At the very least, he'll be bound as he was before."

Once the deed was done, Barnet scowled at Thomas. "The last man we crucified stayed conscious longer than you."

Crucifixion? Dear God. She pointed to the door. "Barnet, go," she commanded, her tone one to be obeyed.

His attention caught to his right. The table by the bed, or more precisely, Thomas's watch. He reached out.

"Leave it. It's mine." She took a step toward him. "You and the men can have all the cargo and the ransom from the crew," she reminded him.

He cast her a disgruntled look and hesitated, then headed out the door, slamming it shut behind him.

Muttering an oath, Catherine returned to the bed.

"Why d-did you s-save my w-watch?" Thomas asked as she spread the covers over his shaking body.

She met his questioning gaze. "This watch obviously

means a great deal to you, just as the Ruby Cross means much to me."

"Ah, you m-mean to hold it in exchange for the cross. It won't work. The sheer p-profit I'll get from the cross outweighs any f-fondness I have for the watch."

Perhaps she'd put his words to the test later. Now she had to get some heat back into him. She exhaled into her hands to warm them up, then began with an arm, rubbing her palms over his skin. "Why didn't you call out to me when the cabin grew so cold?" Was he really that stubborn?

He shook his head, his eyes rolling to the ceiling as if she were half daft. "Wasn't this what you wanted when you s-stripped me of my clothes? Typically when someone desires to f-force information from a prisoner, they th-thrive on opportunities such as this…" He gave her a sidelong glance. "Your quartermaster is r-right to question you. Why are you tending me rather than taking advantage?"

Moving to the other arm, she frowned. "If you'd rather have Barnet have a go at you, I can call him back," she spat. The fool should be silent and accept his good fortune instead of questioning her logic.

Barnet believed she'd been too soft with Thomas, and by all accounts, he was correct, although she couldn't rightly say why. She was accustomed to doing whatever necessary for her family to survive. Now her mother and son were at mortal risk. She should beat Thomas, cut him, hand him over to Barnet, allowing anything short of killing him… She frowned. The mere thought put a sour taste in her mouth.

Was it compassion that kept her from hurting him? Cowardice? Stupidity? Or perhaps none of those. From the first moment they'd met, she'd seen glimpses of the type of man he was. Strong, capable, confident. And the more time she'd spent with him, the more his mischievous nature and keen wit had emerged. In an odd, twisted sort of way, she'd almost enjoyed their sparring. So much so, he'd distracted her from her cause. Curse it.

She had to find some way to make Thomas talk, a method other than causing pain and death. Her gaze caught on his pocket watch still sitting on the table by the bed. How much did he value the piece? Enough to get her what she wanted?

• • •

Although tremors racked him, Thomas had the urge to laugh. His *jailer*, the person in charge of causing him pain and misery, was doing her utmost to save him. She truly had no idea what forcing a prisoner to talk meant. Lucky for him.

"Why does your watch mean so much to you?" she asked, her ministrations moving to his sides. Her hands over the blankets, she rubbed him up and down vigorously.

He shouldn't answer. A skilled torturer could use whatever he said against him. A *skilled* torturer. He smothered a chuckle. Very well. "My father g-gave it to me to commemorate becoming the captain of this ship."

"He must be very proud of you." Catherine was bent over him, her attention on warming him, making his skin tingle and sting as it thawed. Her coat gaped open, exposing her shirt, still untied at the top, providing a glimpse of delectable breasts. The sight heated him far more than the rubbing.

"Y-Yes. My father was proud for a time, but it didn't last." His father's approval had always been fleeting, which, in an odd way, spurred him to greater heights. To feel that admiration again.

"What do you mean?" she asked, her breasts moving in a rhythmic dance as she warmed his chest. Such a curative sight.

"My father thrives on competition. We all do. My b-brothers and I..." His mind stuttered when Catherine turned her ministrations to his hips and thighs. "Perhaps not my mother... Although I suppose she is competitive in her own w-way—hosting parties and events to impress her peers."

The brush of Catherine's hands, even through the bedcovers, stirred his blood, and something else as well. Apparently that region of his body was responding faster than anywhere else. Normally, he might enjoy being tied naked to his bed with a woman caressing him, if he weren't so damn cold.

"In what way do you compete?" she asked.

"In everything. Gambling, w-women, drinking, our occupations, o-our wealth...any success."

"You compete against your family?"

"My brothers mostly." His father wouldn't be nearly as proud if he himself were defeated by a son. "It's how my n-nose was broken, the first time." On a stupid lark in a pub, half drunk.

"Your brothers broke your nose?" She adjusted her position, her hands grazing parts already well warmed.

A groan stuck in his throat, his temperature rising with every stroke. "Just one. Charles. Sparring when we were young. The pub owner made a bit of money, and we got free ale." Seemed like a fair trade at the time, especially over the next week, as he had taunted his brother about losing.

"I don't understand."

Thomas shook his head. If Charles had won, there would have been hell to pay. "Charles will soon be running for the House of Commons, a politician, no less." Once that lump won a position in Parliament, he'd be a tough competitor to beat. "My other brother, Stephen is a solicitor, working toward becoming a barrister, God help us."

Someone knocked on the door, and Catherine rose from the bed. "And you're the captain of a merchantman, working for the Lamont Shipping company."

Yes, he was behind his brothers on that score. "Once I sell the Ruby Cross, I'll work for myself." Then he'd be on more equal footing.

Catherine opened the door. "Arrange a hot bath," she ordered as she accepted a large mug. A bath? Thomas could scarce hear the response, but Catherine's answer was clear, "Do as I say. Be off with you." She shut the door and headed back to the bed, the scent of coffee infusing the cabin. "Do your parents encourage this behavior of competing against your brothers?"

"Why not? They now have a ship's captain, a politician, and a lawyer for sons."

She glanced from the mug in her hand to him and back before snaking an arm beneath his shoulders and propping him up enough so he could take a drink. "Does all this competition make you happy?"

That first taste of hot coffee was like heaven on earth. Dear God. He hadn't realized how much he'd needed a cup. He stopped for a breath of air, warmth traveling to the pit of his stomach. "Why shouldn't it make me happy? Comparing myself to my brothers has driven me to become successful and independent."

"I don't understand why you can't cheer one another's accomplishments rather than make your lives a competition." She helped him to drink more of the brew, and for the first time in a long while, he not only allowed someone's help but relished in their tending. "Are any of your brothers married? Do they have children?" she asked.

Indeed, how nice to have someone tend him and offer comfort…even if that someone had been the cause of his incapacitation. As for his brothers. Married? He gave a laugh. "No. They haven't had time, as of yet." He studied her features, beautiful and kind. What would it be like to have a wife, someone to care when he fell ill or had his nose broken? "Once their careers are established, perhaps finding wives will be the new challenge."

In truth, he'd never questioned his happiness. No time to and no reason to. He had this ship, and soon he'd own one himself. That should make him happy enough.

Catherine set down the coffee on the small table and resumed heating him up, rubbing his arms once more. He could tell her to stop. He would survive, with or without her help. He could tell her that, but he held his tongue and enjoyed her touch instead.

Chapter Four

Catherine's gaze locked onto Thomas, still tied to the bed, as she carried her lunch of pork roast and potatoes into the cabin. She set the meal down on the small table as close to Thomas as possible. He looked far better than he had earlier this morning. Virtually no signs of his near freezing remained.

Thomas eyed the bathtub sitting in the center of the room, the water steaming. Would the promise of a warm bath and a good meal sway him into talking? Unlikely. Although by now he should be hungrier and weaker.

"Shall we take up where we left off?" she asked.

He smiled, his confidence back in top form. "You don't believe tempting me with food will work, do you?"

She squelched the oath tickling the tip of her tongue. He was far too stubborn. "On the contrary. The food is mine." She stabbed a bite of potato from the plate and popped it into her mouth with a grin. Blasted man.

His stomach growled, and some sense of satisfaction rose within her, until he spoke. "My shoulders hurt like the devil. Maybe if you rub the ache away, I might talk." His eyes glowed with mischief. What an arse.

Looking past her, he nodded toward the tub. "The water is getting cold."

"So it is." She had originally ordered the hot bath for him when he'd been shaking so very badly. But at present he appeared healthy and whole, and irritating as ever. Not only did he no longer require a bath for warmth, he didn't deserve one. That and she had no way to keep him bound while he bathed. He'd most likely strangle her the moment his hands were free. She turned to look at the steam rising above the water. After all the trouble the men had gone to, they just might string her up if it went unused. And frankly, she didn't want to let it go to waste.

She rose from the bed and crossed to the tub, then dipped her fingers into the water, yearning to step inside and sink into the luxurious heat. Catherine looked back at Thomas. He watched her with curiosity.

"You didn't think this bath was for you, did you?" she teased.

A smile lifted the corner of his lips. "Feel free to partake. I don't mind."

Indeed. He wouldn't mind having her strip naked before him. So what to do with him? She couldn't bathe in front of him, and asking to have him removed from the cabin would place him right in Barnet's hands. She headed to the armoire. No reason to send him away when she could simply obstruct his view. Opening the tall wardrobe, she scanned the contents. She'd seen it earlier. Aye. She retrieved a white cravat from inside and returned to the bed.

Thomas smirked. "What are you planning? Usually I don a full suit when I wear my cravat."

"Not today." She covered his eyes with the long cloth, wrapping it around his head and tying it off at the side. "There. Now off to my bath."

"There's soap near the basin on the corner table," he offered. Why, she had no idea. She'd been torturing him for nigh on two days, or attempting to, at least. No matter. She found the soap and returned to the tub, where she released the buttons of her coat and slipped the fabric from her shoulders, her every sound magnified in the silence.

"Your coat," Thomas said as he lay still in the bed.

"What?"

"You're removing your surcoat," he explained.

True, but why did he bother to point it out? She slipped off one boot and set it on the floor.

"Did you remove your left or right boot?" he asked.

She paid no heed to him and his nonsense, and pulled off her other one.

"I would guess you'll cast off your breeches next."

Catherine halted with her hands on the opening to her breeches. What was he doing? And why? The slight chill to the air had little to do with the bumps rising on her skin. Thomas couldn't see her. He only guessed by sound what clothing she removed. Even so, she couldn't seem to catch her breath. Purely out of spite, she shed her stockings, leaving her breeches in place.

"Ah, I was wrong. The sound was so quiet, it must have been your hose."

"Stop that!"

"Why?" he laughed. "It amuses me, and apparently irritates you…which amuses me all the more."

"It doesn't irritate me. Do what you must," she muttered. *Doesn't irritate me at all.* She released the buttons and slipped the breeches down her legs, the slide of fabric over her thighs more stirring than it ought to be. She flung the breeches aside.

"All that remains is your shirt, then you'll be as naked as I am."

Don't listen to him. She shivered as the tails of the shirt rode up the length of her body in a sweeping brush of cotton on skin. She dropped the shirt to the floor.

"Just the two of us naked and alone." His voice charmed and tempted. Damn him.

Catherine stepped into the tub. "Your first mate is recovering from his illness," she blurted, eager to change the subject. She sank into the tub so fast, water splashed over the sides.

"Is he?"

"Aye," she breathed.

"How's the water?"

"*Mmm.*" She relaxed back, savoring the all-encompassing warmth.

"I don't need my sight to imagine you leaning against the rim, your shoulders just above the surface, a pleased smile on your face."

She growled low in her throat. If only he would stop talking, she might enjoy her bath.

"Your hair is growing damp, and your skin is taking on a rosy glow as the water touches you, caresses you."

Glancing down, she noted her pinkened skin, the water washing over her breasts in a tantalizing dance. A need she'd long suppressed swept through her from her chest to her belly. She clamped down on those dangerous feelings. She was supposed to be abusing him, not the other way round. "Be quiet, or I'll run you through with my sword."

"I'd much rather run you through with mine," he suggested, his voice a sexy rumble that made her shiver.

Oh! She dunked her head in the water, eager to drown out anything more he might say. Giving her hair a good scrubbing with the soap, she could only hear the scrape of her fingers along her scalp. Bliss. She rinsed, then retrieved the soap again and ran it over one arm.

"How does my soap feel against your skin?" he asked, a smile in his tone.

She squeezed her eyes shut. How did he know? Enough of this. Her eyes sprang open, and determination straightened her spine. He wouldn't best her. No, she'd take up the challenge. "The texture is rough, but the scent is clean," she responded. "It feels good as I slide it over my neck and shoulders, now the length of my arms… *Mmm*, my chest and belly." Did her words affect him as much as they did her? Her breasts ached. His silence was encouraging. If nothing else, she'd put his taunts to rest, at least for the moment. She added a soft groan for good measure.

She could see no discernible effect on him. No, wait. A slight flare of his nostrils. She sighed and tried anew. "You were right. My hair is damp, dangling and dripping onto my bare shoulders." She lifted her leg, sending water trickling back into the tub. "Now to clean my legs, one at a time, thoroughly, from my toes to my thighs."

Watching him closely, she detected no reaction. Damn. Then again, he was a well-trained competitor, one who would hide her effect on him even if he had to bite off his own tongue to distract himself. "Are you jealous?" she asked him.

"Of what?" he responded, his voice strained.

"Do you wish you were in this tub with me?"

He said nothing. No teasing. No glib remark. Smiling, she rose from the tub and grabbed up the towel. Perhaps it was time to discover just how much control this man had.

. . .

A rush of water. Cloth rubbing against skin. The padding of bare feet across the floor. Dear God. Catherine was heading toward the bed, toward him. Taut with anticipation, Thomas waited for a sign she was close. There. The clean scent of soap, mingled with the warm and alluring aroma of woman. The mattress beside him dipped, and he could feel her shiver.

"The air is cool," she whispered, her breath hot against his cheek. "My skin is covered in bumps...and peaks."

The sultry rasp of her voice sank into his skin and rushed straight to his groin as he imagined the *peaks* she spoke of. Stiff, rosy peaks he yearned to taste and tease.

She trailed her fingers over his stubbled jaw, down his neck to his chest. "You thought to taunt me," she breathed, "but who is in control now?"

The bedcovers moved lower, baring more of his chest, then his abdomen, almost to his erection, which threatened to throw off the rest of the bedding on its own. Perhaps he'd been foolish to taunt her. After all, he was the one tied to the bed. But in his defense, he'd enjoyed every minute. Until now. Now his body conspired against him, especially when he imagined how she must look hovering over him, scantily clad, still damp from the bathwater. Maybe her torturing skills weren't as poor as he'd originally thought.

Her hand strayed to the side of his pelvis, exploring him in leisurely strokes. She was close. So close, her breath tickled his lips. Ah, the memory of those lush lips, soft and full. He couldn't stop himself… He needed… Thomas pulled against the ropes securing his wrists to the bed and lifted himself up, intent on capturing her lips with his. When he met nothing but air, he uttered a foul curse and dropped back onto the mattress. *Wicked woman!*

She untied the knot at the side of his head and removed the blindfold. Her eyes glowed with satisfaction, and a smug smile adorned her lips. Anger burned deep inside his chest. He should have been able to resist her. Instead, he admired the way her damp shirt clung to her breasts, his cock stiff as a marlinespike. This would stop, and it would stop at once. "Let me guess. If I tell you where I've hidden the cross, you'll spread your legs for me?" He cocked a brow and raked his gaze over her. "Or maybe you'll spread them without such information."

Catherine's eyes widened, and she slapped him across the face. A hearty smack that made his cheek sting. "Don't ever talk to me in such a way again," she bit out as she rose to her feet. Her eyes flashed with anger and a hint of something more. Hurt? She turned her back to him and hurried to dress.

He had the urge to apologize for his caustic words. An urge he thrust aside. He was a prisoner here, and as such, he had every right to use whatever means necessary against his captor. He had no reason to feel guilty.

Then why do I?

Someone rapped hard on the door. Catherine quickly donned her boots and strode across the room. Barnet stood outside, scowling as if he'd been wronged.

"I've heard tell that you're bathin' the prisoner," he shouted into her face. "Tell me the rumor is false." The quartermaster looked past Catherine to the tub, and his features darkened all the more.

Catherine shook her head. "He was not the one in the—"

Seizing her by the hair, Barnet jerked her head back, and Thomas yanked against his ropes, to do what, he wasn't sure. "Your hair is damp," Barnet growled. "You took a bath with Glanville in the room!"

She pulled her dagger from her belt and settled the tip against Barnet's belly. "Let. Go of me. Now."

Barnet glanced at his offending hand as if surprised at what he'd done. He released her. "Catherine—"

"You are not my brother, husband, or father," she ground out. "What I do is of no concern to you."

"I only care about your well-bein'. It's obvious somethin' is goin' on between you and him," Barnet said between clenched teeth.

Catherine raised her hand to stop him from going on and tucked her blade back into her belt. "Yes, I bathed with him in the room, but he wore a blindfold." She moved to the bed and lifted the cravat. "See?"

Barnet's features softened to some extent. A pity. What would Barnet do to Catherine if he knew the whole truth of what had transpired during her bath?

No doubt, he wouldn't have to worry about being under her control anymore. Of course, then he'd have to contend with Barnet. In comparison, he'd much prefer Catherine.

Her voluptuous curves came to mind. Yes, much preferable.

As if Barnet had heard his thoughts, the quartermaster settled a glare on Thomas. "It's time I handled this interrogation. He should have confessed the location of the cross by now."

Catherine rolled her shoulders back as if readying for a fight. "No, he's *my* prisoner."

Barnet's scarred lip thinned. "Your methods are soft. This can't go on. We'll be in London two days hence."

"But—"

"Or have you forgotten your son so soon?"

Catherine stood motionless, stunned.

"You have till morning. Then your prisoner is mine," Barnet snarled. "We have no more time to spare." With that, he turned and walked away, the discussion at an end.

Catherine stared after him for the longest time, then sighed and shut the door. "He's right." Her dark brown eyes sought his. "You need to tell me where the Ruby Cross is. Now."

"Or what?"

"Or Barnet will hurt you, badly."

"I'm not afraid of Barnet or pain." In fact, the first ship he commissioned once he sold the cross would be named *Barnet* in the quartermaster's *honor*.

"You're a fool. Is the cross worth your life?" she asked in earnest. "If you give him too much trouble, Barnet will kill you when he's through."

Thomas shrugged. "He won't kill me if he wants the cross."

She threw up her hands with a look of disbelief. "It's *me* who wants it. Not him." She turned to pace the floor. "He has a temper. If he gets angry enough, he will kill you, and then neither you nor I will get the cross."

"So be it." He'd faced challenges his whole life, and he'd be damned if he'd back away from this one.

"You don't mean what you say. No object, no matter how valuable, is worth your life." She worried her lower lip, and it almost looked as if tears glistened in her eyes, but they were gone before he could tell for sure.

Why would she cry? Because of the cross? Unlikely. She seemed too pragmatic to weep over a lost relic. She hadn't appeared frightened of Barnet, despite his actions, although maybe she should be. "If anyone has a reason to worry about Barnet, it's you."

Her brow furrowed. "Why would you think that?"

Was she blind? "It's obvious he's infatuated with you. And if he's a man with a temper…"

Catherine shook her head. "We've been friends for years." Although a flicker of unease crossed her face.

The way Barnet looked at her wasn't as a friend. "Your husband is gone. Perhaps he wants to take his place."

She waved the thought away. "He knows I have no interest in him. Tell me. Where is the cross?"

"After days of being bound in my own cabin, why would I tell you now?" She'd clearly lost her mind.

Her gazed bored into him. "If you don't, I'll tell your employer, Gordon Lamont, you're using his vessel for your own personal pursuits, shipping and selling priceless antiquities."

His stomach clenched. "He won't care." *Would he?*

"I doubt he'll be getting a share of the profits…and he is a man of business."

Which had been the main reason he hadn't bothered

to ask permission. "I'll take the risk." Besides, Catherine couldn't contact Lamont before they reached port. She was no threat at this very moment.

She must have realized the same thing judging from her frown and the way she scanned the cabin, searching for something. "What are you afraid of?" she mumbled. "Apparently not death." She speared him with a look. "The death of a loved one. Everyone fears that."

Somehow he couldn't take the comment seriously, not from her. "Are you threatening my family?"

Catherine looked away, rather than answering. Just as he'd thought—she wouldn't hurt an innocent. Her attention returned to him, and anger flared in her eyes. "Don't look so smug. I could always threaten your manhood."

And here he'd thought she'd been coming to like his manhood. Still, when she approached the bed with a determined expression on her face, his balls itched and sweat beaded on his forehead…until she reached toward the table and retrieved the pocket watch his father had given him. The lump forming in his throat was about the same size as the piece she dangled in front of him.

"How much does this watch mean to you?" she asked.

He swallowed. "It's only a watch." Although one of the few gifts his father had ever given him, it wouldn't hold him back. Perhaps he'd get another soon, when he showed his father a newly acquired ship.

"You don't care if I destroy the piece then."

"No." He nearly choked on the word.

She opened the lid and set it on the floor, then raised her foot, her booted heel ready to crush the glass and all that lay beneath.

Thomas held his breath. He would have other watches, other displays of pride from his father.

"You're sure?" She stared deeply in his eyes as if somehow she knew how much the damn watch meant to him.

He nodded once. He could do no more.

She brought her foot down hard and he winced, waiting to hear breaking glass. It didn't come. Cursing beneath her breath, Catherine retrieved the watch from the floor and closed the lid, then slipped it into the pocket of her breeches. "No sense destroying a perfectly good watch."

Relief washed through him, and with it, gratitude. How stupid. Grateful to his tormentor. Tormentor. *Ha.* Catherine was too soft for this kind of work, and although he was glad for it, he had a feeling she would pay dearly for her failings. The true test for them both was surely yet to come.

Chapter Five

Catherine awoke in a daze to a slight tug on her wrist. She'd fallen asleep? Last thing she remembered was singing a horrific discordant rendition of *Greensleeves*, her voice becoming so hoarse her throat ached as she attempted to keep Thomas alert and annoyed enough to spill his secret. The annoyance part worked. The keeping him awake part… She'd even failed to keep herself from falling asleep.

Her other arm was raised far to the side and over her head, and something rough encompassed her wrist. She opened her eyes with a start. What in God's name…?

Thomas leaned over her, still unclothed, and tied the rope around her wrist to the bedpost. He greeted her with a dazzling smile, those green eyes of his glinting in the lamplight. "Good morning, lovely."

"I don't understand. How?" She spied his wrists, rubbed raw from his escape.

He pressed down on her encumbered arms and bent

close. "How does it feel to be the one in restraints?"

"I'm not afraid of you," she croaked out. She should be frightened—he could do with her whatever he wanted. No, he wouldn't hurt her. Somehow she was sure of that fact. Humiliation was much more likely, and of that she had no fear. She lived in the Rookery of St. Giles, the most squalid district in all of London. A place of sickness and filth, open sewers running through the streets, with prostitutes and reprobates walking the alleys at all hours of the day and night. She had no pride left to damage. "I have nothing you want. There's no need to torture me."

He chuckled, his face relaxed, almost gleeful. "Ah Catherine, you truly don't understand torture, do you? Some of us do it simply for amusement…or revenge."

Her throat grew tight, and her mind raced through all she'd done to him. She'd never caused him pain. No food or water. She could survive that, and she wouldn't have to for long. Thomas was outnumbered. As soon as someone came to the cabin, he'd be recaptured and she would be free. What else? Terrible singing…and… Thomas's eyes smoldered, scorching her from the inside out. Oh Lord. She had taunted him with her body, with her touch. She'd stripped him naked. Just the thought of him doing the same made her pulse leap and her skin tingle. "You'll be caught soon, so take heed. There will be repercussions for whatever you do to me."

Her heart stuttered a beat. Once Thomas was a prisoner again, Barnet would have a go at him. By tonight, Thomas might be dead. "Tell me where you've hidden the cross," she whispered, knowing full well she had no authority to make such a demand.

Thomas's grin only widened. "The sun won't rise for

several hours. Plenty of time for me to have some fun." He bent forward and his lips took possession of hers in a leisurely kiss that savored and teased. This certainly didn't feel like torment. He tasted warm and masculine. Her mouth moved with his and their tongues entwined. In the span of a minute, all trace of leisure dissipated, replaced by a frenzy of desire and need.

His hands traveled from her arms to cup her face before heading lower to cover her breasts. Even through her shirt, his caresses melted her insides and had her gasping for breath. He plucked at her nipple, his groan warm on her lips, and she arched into him, craving more. Her body welcomed his exploration as if it had waited for this moment since they'd met. His erection, hard and thick, pressed into her thigh, and she pulled against her restraints, desperate to move closer, to feel more of him. She whimpered when her arms couldn't obey.

"Ah, God," Thomas moaned as he tore himself from her and raked a hand through his hair. His breathing ragged, he sat back and stared at her. Never had she felt so vulnerable as this moment with his fiery gaze boring into hers. He shook his head. "I'm not sure who's torturing whom here." He slid off the bed and strode to the armoire without another word.

Her only thought was to call him back, but apparently she did have some pride left. "Where will you go?" she asked instead. "Your ship has been overrun. You have no hope of escape."

He tugged on a pair of black breeches. "I know this ship from bow to stern. I'll find a way to release my men and get the upper hand."

His confidence knew no bounds. Could he really

accomplish so much all on his own? And if he did, what of her son and mother? The fear came at last with a chill and a shiver. "I need the cross."

Thomas's look was one of disdain before he pulled a shirt over his head.

"Please. My son and mother are being held for ransom. I need the Ruby Cross to free them. There's no other way." Her heart ached with the need to make him listen, and yet, her pleas fell on deaf ears. Thomas didn't so much as acknowledge her as he finished dressing, then retrieved her sword and dagger from beside the bed, tucking them into his belt.

He reached over and slipped his fingers into the pocket of her breeches. His watch. He withdrew the timepiece and tucked it into his own pocket.

"Please," she said once more, "help me save my son."

Thomas arched a brow and picked up the cravat she'd used to blindfold him. "Why would I believe you? And after being imprisoned in this cabin, why should I care?"

"But—"

He stuffed the cravat into her mouth, silencing her, and crossed to the door. After peering out, he spared one look back and left the cabin, shutting the door behind him.

A vision of Jonas, her sweet boy, flashed inside her head—his hair as dark as her own and his lean face smudged with dirt as he tried to make her laugh with his silly expressions. He'd never failed to cheer her no matter the cause of her worry. Dear Jonas…and her mother, a woman dedicated to her family, but too weak to do much more than sit and stitch.

Thomas would be recaptured. He had to be. And when he was, she would find a way to save the two people who mattered most in her life.

• • •

Finally outside that wretched cabin, Thomas took in a deep breath of fresh air, savoring his freedom for a long minute and letting the November breeze cool his blood. His attempt at retribution had failed miserably. Aye, Catherine had writhed beneath him, her passion stoked to a blaze, but he, too, had felt the burn. In those moments, he'd wanted to release her from her bonds and sate them both as he would a cherished lover. Not exactly what he'd had in mind for the woman who'd held him captive these last two days. In fact, as he'd worked to pull his hand from the rope, he'd thought of how he would cut off her clothes as she'd done to him. But when the opportunity arose, he hadn't been able to do the deed. All he could think of was how defenseless she'd be—naked and bound—for whatever man found her first. Like Barnet.

No matter what Catherine believed, Barnet's feelings for her ran deep. And considering how eager the man had been to flay him alive for the attention she'd bestowed on him, she'd best be wary. Not that he should care one whit.

Thomas glanced up at the lookout, where the lone guard stood watch. The moon's hazy glow outlined the pirate's movements. Thomas stayed in the shadows and moved toward the door to the galley, the easiest and likely most deserted path to the hold. Looking for his men in the bowels of the ship was probably a fool's errand. No doubt, the pirate ship would be better equipped than this one to keep prisoners. But when he'd been captured, Catherine had ordered her crew to take his men to the hold of *this* ship, although the reasoning behind her command made little sense.

He had a couple of hours before the majority of the pirates would be awake and about. Why not verify his suspicions? Besides, walking the decks... Hell, walking at all, was heaven.

If his men were indeed being detained below, he could free them by attacking the guards, then he and his crew could take back their ship. He paused in the galley and snatched up a loaf of bread, biting into it with zeal. While he could tolerate the hunger pangs, he'd need his strength. Likewise, he found a bucket of water and drank his fill.

Aye, they were still outnumbered at least two to one, but the pirates had split their crew between the two vessels. With a surprise attack, he and his men might be able to defeat the pirates here before fighting the rest.

Food in his stomach and an eagerness in his step, he ventured down into the belly of the ship, his hands riding the weapons in his belt and his memory guiding him in the darkness. They wouldn't have weapons, but his men could make do. Many of the tools aboard would serve just as well as a dagger or sword. Marlinespikes, normally used for rope work, were in great abundance.

He reached the hold and stopped. No lanterns for the guards and deathly quiet. Warily, Thomas ventured farther. No barrels or crates. He made a thorough inspection of the entire area. Nothing at all. No sign of his men, and all of the cargo and supplies were gone. He blew out a long breath. Maybe not as he'd hoped, but just as he'd thought. Damn. Now what?

His men were likely on the *Sea Sprite*, the ship they sailed behind. He could capture Barnet and order him to release all prisoners, but he didn't relish the odds. Just him with his two hostages against a ship full of pirates. Did they care for Barnet and Catherine enough to do as he ordered? Or would they fight him, come what may? He couldn't take that chance. Which left Catherine. He suspected Barnet would do anything for her. Better yet, she was already a prisoner.

Thomas retraced his steps, the bread he'd eaten souring in his stomach. If he used Catherine against Barnet, he'd have to threaten to hurt her, perhaps cause her pain to prove to Barnet he was willing. Bloody hell. The idea shouldn't trouble him after all she'd done—capturing his ship, holding him prisoner, humiliating him at every turn. He should be angry with her, glad to see her suffer, and to be the one who would administer her pain. But he wasn't.

He never hurt women, and Catherine… He rubbed a hand over the back of his neck. Aside from bruising his pride, she hadn't caused him any real harm. In fact, she'd gone to great lengths to ensure his safety. She'd kept Barnet from torturing him in the true sense. She'd cared for him when he'd nearly frozen to death. He huffed out a laugh. Even before then, he'd known she had a kind soul. In truth, he'd been tempted to call out to her when the cold had become too much. It had been his pride that had kept him silent. Indeed, his time as her prisoner had proven to be almost enjoyable at times, a challenging and stimulating game.

He would spare her if he could, but sadly, he had no choice. To save his men and his ship, he would use her against Barnet. Thomas strode to his cabin and opened the door. He took several steps before the sight before him registered.

Catherine stood with her back to him, and quickly spun around. *Free? But how?*

A heavy click behind him gave him the answer. He glanced over his shoulder at Barnet sitting at the corner table. He had a pistol pointed at Thomas's spine.

"Figured you'd return soon, you dog." Barnet rose from the table, the gleam in his eyes one of a man bent on vengeance.

Catherine stepped forward, "Barnet, we've discussed this. He didn't force himself on me."

Thomas studied her but detected no trace of the lie. In a sense, he *had* forced himself on her. He just hadn't finished the deed.

Barnet closed the distance between them, the barrel of his pistol nudging Thomas's back. "I came here early this mornin', eager to finally make you talk. But alas, Catherine still won't let me lay a hand on you. Why is that?" Barnet demanded.

"Enough," Catherine scolded Barnet. Her expression turned grave, and she looked Thomas in the eye. "I will give you one more chance to tell me where I can find the Ruby Cross."

"Or what?"

She lifted her chin a notch and crossed her arms over her chest. "If you don't give me what I want, I will sink this ship and the cross with it."

"You won't." The cross meant too much to her to risk losing it forever.

"Believe me, I will if you force my hand."

"Then consider it forced." She was lying. She had to be. And he would wait for her to come to her senses. His pride would allow nothing else.

Mere hours later, Thomas stood beside Barnet on the main deck as Catherine poured a second bottle of rum onto the planks. The damn woman.

"This is your last chance to save your ship." The determined set to Catherine's jaw didn't fool him. *She won't do it. She wants the cross as much as I do.*

It had to be true, and yet his heart pounded hard all the same. He peered out over the decks of the *Argo Navis*, the ship he'd captained for more than a year. Captain. He didn't take the title lightly. He'd worked hard to get where he was. His hands strayed to the watch in his pocket, a commemoration of his achievement.

The *Sea Sprite* floated some fifty yards away, all aboard save himself, Catherine, and Barnet, whose pistol had been in his hand since Thomas's recapture.

That same weapon pointed at him now. "If you sink my ship, you'll never get the cross," Thomas warned, his muscles so tense his shoulders ached.

Uncertainty flickered over Catherine's features like a candle's flame disturbed by a slight breeze. It vanished just as quickly. "I'm sincerely sorry for what I'm about to do. This is a fine vessel."

"Don't go apologizin' to the likes of him," Barnet insisted. "Just do what you have to do."

Catherine nodded and extended the smoldering linstock to the pool of rum spilled on the decking. Thomas's breath caught in his throat.

No. She wouldn't. He took a step toward her, and Barnet grabbed him by the shoulder, holding him back.

Catherine touched the staff's forked end to the rum and a blaze erupted, spreading over the liquid in a dance he couldn't tear his gaze from. Thomas's stomach hit the decking, then rage rushed to the fore. The flames quickly rose, consuming sail and wood. His ship would soon be lost. *Dammit. Dammit. Dammit!*

He turned to Catherine, his hands itching to strangle her. "You bitch!"

Catherine's eyes flared wide.

"Stay back," Barnet ordered, his pistol aimed at Thomas's chest.

"As captain, *I'm* in charge of this ship. She's mine to care for, and you've…you've…" Raw fury tightened his throat as he watched the crackling flames climb higher and higher.

She tossed the linstock into the fire. "Get the cross, or it will go down with the *Argo Navis*."

"Go to hell!" The Ruby Cross would never be hers.

Barnet grinned. "Do as she says or stay here and die." Judging by the broad flash of teeth, Barnet hoped he'd choose the latter.

Tempting. If nothing more than out of spite. The Ruby Cross was the key to his future, the means to garner his family's admiration and respect.

"Thomas," Catherine warned. "We don't have much time."

Already the fire had scorched a fair portion of the main deck and climbed halfway up the masts, the heat sweltering. He desperately wanted to stand firm, to refuse them access to their prize, but common sense prevailed. Dying would help no one. Besides, if the cross wasn't at the bottom of the sea, he had a chance to steal it back. "Very well. Follow me."

He led them away from the main deck to his cabin, black smoke rising over their heads to obscure the clear morning sky. He stepped inside his quarters, and Catherine's brow wrinkled.

"It can't be in here. I searched this entire room."

He smirked. "I can't tell you how much I enjoyed seeing you so close to what you wanted. Oblivious the whole time." He walked to the ornate panel at the head of the bed and pressed what would appear to be one of many round ornamental carvings. A secret compartment slid free from the elaborate front, and he retrieved the Ruby Cross from within.

Heavy in his hand, the gold shimmered and the rubies glistened. An image of his own ship, tall and proud, clouded his vision, along with the look of pride in his father's eyes and the envy on his brothers' faces. The scent of smoke invaded his senses, and he coughed on the now hazy air.

A hand snatched the cross from his clutches—Catherine, the ship-burning thief he longed to throw overboard. "Let's go," she said, leading the way out of the cabin, holding a corner of her shirt over her mouth. Since he'd rather not be broiled alive, Thomas followed, with Barnet the last to leave. He heard the strength of the fire long before he saw the blaze. The roar was deafening. His eyes stinging, he, too, covered his mouth.

Once on deck, the sight that greeted him punched him in the gut. A wall of flames stretched to the topmost mast, and the smoke, thick and black, converged into a billowing cloud that blotted out the sun. They hurried toward the ladder that would take them down to the rowboat, the heat almost unbearable.

A resounding crack brought Thomas up short, and his gaze sought the source. The mainmast. Damaged by cannon fire when they'd first fought these vermin, the thick mast crashed toward the deck…and Catherine. *No!* He leaped forward, grabbed her about the waist, and flung them both out of the way. They landed hard, his body protecting hers as the fiery timber smashed into the decking behind them.

"Catherine." He carefully rolled her to her side and brushed the hair from her face. Her eyes were closed, but she breathed.

"Get your hands off her!" Barnet rose to his feet, his pistol still aimed in Thomas's direction. The idiot.

"I just saved her, for God's sake," Thomas grumbled, coughing against the smoke that grew thicker by the moment. "And she's unconscious. Unless you'd like to stow your weapon, I'll have to carry her to the boat."

Barnet hesitated a heart's beat, his glance dropping to his weapon. No doubt wondering if Thomas would throw him into the fire if given a chance. Extremely tempting.

Waving the pistol, Barnet nodded. "Pick her up," he choked out.

Discreetly, Thomas retrieved the cross from where it had tumbled onto the deck. *Welcome back, lovely.* Then he lifted Catherine's limp body in his arms. He headed to the ladder along the side of the ship, but Barnet stopped him with a raised hand. "I'll go first."

Of course he would. Barnet disappeared over the side, and Thomas rested Catherine on the deck a moment while he slid the cross beneath his shirt and into the waist of his breeches. Lifting her once more, he stared down at

Catherine's serene face. He had the cross, and he had Catherine. If there was any way to escape, he would do it now and take her with him. She needed to be taught a lesson about angering the wrong people, and he was just the man to teach her. Unfortunately, any manner of escape eluded him, so he adjusted his hold on her, hoisting her to his shoulder. He climbed over the ship's side and descended to the boat.

Two of the *Sea Sprite's* crewmen waited with Barnet below, ready to man the oars. Barnet's bloody pistol following his every move, Thomas stepped into the boat and sat, depositing Catherine in his lap.

"Set her over here," Barnet demanded, indicating an open spot to his left.

Somewhat reluctantly, he did as he was told. Barnet examined the bump on Catherine's head before patting her pockets and inspecting her coat. Finding nothing, he turned on Thomas. "Where's the Ruby Cross?"

He looked back toward the *Argo Navis*. "She must have lost it in the fall."

"Like hell," Barnet snarled. "Hold him," he ordered the two crewmen, who stopped rowing to do as commanded.

Thomas didn't fight them as they restrained his arms. Where would he go? The ocean would only provide a temporary escape.

Barnet stowed his weapon in his belt. He made short work of checking Thomas's pockets, then searched his waist, quickly finding the cross.

Thomas stifled a curse.

"You bastard," Barnet spat. He ripped Thomas's shirt from his breeches and seized the antiquity. Barnet slid the Ruby Cross into his waistcoat pocket, his glare still burning bright. Before Thomas could blink, Barnet reared his arm back and landed a blow to Thomas's ribs.

Uttering a grunt, Thomas doubled over as pain radiated through his abdomen. This time he did fight for freedom from the two pirates holding him, eager to defend himself if there was more to come.

Barnet's pistol came back into view. "Stay still, or I'll kill you where you sit."

Every muscle tense, Thomas sat motionless and waited. Would Barnet shoot no matter if he followed the command or not?

Catherine groaned and opened her eyes. "Barnet?" When she spied the pirates holding Thomas and the look of fury on Barnet's face, she gasped and gripped Barnet's arm. "Don't!"

Barnet stared at Thomas a long minute, then glanced at Catherine and returned to his seat. "Row," he barked out.

His men took up the oars and set off.

Anger blazed through Thomas's veins as he watched the *Argo Navis* crumble and burn in front of his very eyes. Damn Catherine and Barnet.

This battle may have been lost, but the war wasn't over. Somehow, someway, he would get the cross back and make them both pay for their treachery.

Chapter Six

"Bring Glanville to me," Catherine ordered one of her crewmen as she headed for her cabin aboard the *Sea Sprite*. She crossed the sizable quarters and sank into a chair at the table, where a feast had already been laid out. Hard to believe just months ago her husband had sat in this same chair, at this same table, in this pitiful cabin. She scanned Peter's sparse quarters, a room filled with only the barest essentials—a bed, an old trunk, and this small table. So different than the captain's cabin she'd been in of late, albeit those hadn't been the quarters of a pirate.

Her husband had never sent home the money he'd promised to make when he'd gone off to sea. And as she'd struggled to feed their son, she'd come to resent Peter, believing he lived well while they barely made ends meet. That he'd left them to escape the squalor they lived in. She'd resented him despite the many times she'd dreamed of doing the same.

Not until she'd set sail with his crew on this voyage, did she realize how little he and his men had. Perhaps her bitterness had been misguided, and Peter's intentions had been genuine, just ill-placed.

Catherine touched the sensitive bump on her head and sucked in a breath. A small price to pay, considering she could have died. Thomas had saved her life. Even after she'd set his ship to blaze. And yet, somehow his actions didn't surprise her. He was an honorable man. Although he teased and annoyed, when he'd had his chance at retribution with her tied to his bed, he hadn't taken advantage. He'd walked away. Men like him were a rarity where she came from.

Movement outside the door drew her attention. Thomas, escorted by two crewmen. Still covered in soot and a wary expression on his face, he stepped through the doorway, his gaze measuring her intentions.

"Let him go," she told the crewmen.

They glanced at each other with questioning looks, and one spoke up. "Are you sure, Cap'n? He's unchained."

"Aye." She stood and pulled her dagger from her belt, the cross safely hidden away. "I can defend myself, if need be." Her brother had trained her well. "Now wait outside, both of you."

Although hesitant, the crewmen nodded and left.

She passed by Thomas and closed the door. "There," she sighed. "Now then. Are you hungry?" She almost winced, remembering how she'd taunted him with those same words. She pointed toward the table laden with stew, bread, and cheese. A basin for washing sat on a small table nearby. "Please, clean up and eat."

His wariness remained, but he made use of the water

and towel, cleaning the remains of the fire from his skin. "Why are you offering me food?"

"You saved my life. The least I can do is provide a decent meal." After all, she'd starved him for days.

He shrugged. "I acted purely on instinct, I assure you."

His words stung, pricking something soft inside her chest. She held back a frown. What had she expected after all she'd done to him? "Even so"—she tucked her dagger into her belt and joined him at the table—"thank you."

Thomas sat and tasted the stew, then scowled. "Venison."

How could he find fault with the choice of meat? She'd eaten a bowl of stew herself, and had found it quite tasty. Aye, venison was a meat few could afford, a luxury.

He sniffed the contents of the mug provided, and his scowl grew darker. "Ale… How kind of you to offer me food and drink stolen from my own ship."

Oh. He was right on that count. Still, the prisoners in the hold weren't eating nearly as well. "I can call someone to take you back to the cell if you wish," she bit out. On any given day she'd dreamed of such food and had gone hungry far more often than she filled her belly.

He ripped off a chunk of bread. "That won't be necessary." Now that he'd had his grumble, he tore into the food like he'd been starved. Which he had. Poor man. She should try to remember how he'd been wronged. The cross was rightfully his, obtained by legal means. Or so she assumed. "How did you come to be in possession of the Ruby Cross?" Maybe he wasn't as innocent as she'd thought.

"What does it matter?"

"It doesn't, except…"

He cocked an eyebrow. "Except what?"

"How do I know you didn't steal the cross?" She gestured toward him. "For all your griping about your circumstances, you may be a thief yourself."

A spark of anger brightened his green eyes. "A friend of mine in Jerusalem discovered the cross in a small crumbling church."

"And he simply gave you a priceless relic?"

"He's a merchant I've worked with before. We'll split the profits as we always do." He dropped his spoon into the bowl. "I'm nothing like you," he spat. "I'm no thief."

She bristled. "Not like me. I would agree with you." She crossed the room, no destination in mind. The furnishings around her, no matter how sparse and worn, were far better than what she had at home. "You have wealth and position. Hell, you grew up with it. Your children will have everything they need to be successful, whereas my son…" Dear Jonas. "Such an unlucky boy to have me for a mother," she muttered. "I can barely provide for him. And aye, I have resorted to thievery when all else has failed."

Each day she had prayed for a miracle. She wanted nothing more than to ensure his future, one far away from St. Giles. A future in which he didn't need to worry he'd have to forgo a meal or wear ill-fitting clothes until they were nothing but rags.

The sympathy washing over Thomas's aristocratic features only roused her anger ever more. Although he wasn't at fault for her station in life, he epitomized everything she wished she had. "Eat your meal."

He paid no heed to her suggestion, his lips thinning. "Now that you have the Ruby Cross, I'd imagine your life will become even better than mine."

"Perhaps, if I sold the piece, but I'll be using it to free my son and my mother."

He cocked his head to the side. "You were telling the truth about why you needed the cross?"

"Aye." If only that weren't the case. "Finally, you believe me?"

"The Ruby Cross is in your possession now. You have no reason to lie." He met her gaze, the look in his eyes sincere. "For what it's worth, I'm sorry to hear your family is at risk."

As was she. A familiar ache tightened her chest. She thrust her rising sadness aside and headed to the old trunk in the corner. "You can have some clean clothes. These might be a bit large, but they'll do." Despite his poor luck as a pirate, her husband had managed to put on weight.

"More gifts? You must be feeling terribly guilty about sinking my ship."

"Hardly," she lied. She'd had no choice but to do what had to be done. A motto she proved true every day.

Thomas stood and walked toward her, no doubt to claim the fresh clothing. "Tell me. How did you know I would hand over the cross instead of letting it sink with the *Argo Navis*?" he asked.

"I'll admit, it was a risk. But after talking with you these last days, I believe I've come to know how you think." She rifled through the trunk and procured a pair of breeches and a shirt.

"Is that so? And how do I think?" he asked from close behind her, his low, smooth tone sending a shiver along her spine.

How could this man affect her so readily? She thrust aside the notion and faced him, holding out the garments.

"You admitted you care more for the cross than the watch your father gave you, even though it's apparent the piece means much to you. Add to that your competitive nature…" She stifled a laugh. "Even now, you most likely believe you'll find a way to get the cross back."

Annoyance burned bright in his green eyes for an instant before his lips twitched into a smile, the annoyance replaced by challenge. In a movement as quick as a flash of steel, he pulled her close, his mouth on hers demanding and possessive. The contact jolted through her, making her pulse race and her legs wobble.

The clothing she held slipped from her hand and dropped to the floor unheeded as she became immersed in the heady sensations he inspired within her. Warmth radiated from her chest and spread through her limbs, desire inflaming her entire being.

He drew away, his arms around her waist, and she groaned at the loss. A smug grin widened his tempting lips. "Are you sure you know me as well as you think? It seems I can still surprise you."

So it appeared. She stiffened. He'd kissed her solely to prove a point? She peered more deeply into his eyes. No, the heat she saw there had nothing to do with reason. Hell, she didn't care his reasons. With a swift movement of her own, she launched herself onto her toes and pressed her mouth to his, eager to let the feel of his kiss carry her away from reality again. He didn't disappoint. His arms about her tightened, his hands delving beneath her surcoat to roam over her back. Only the thin layer of her linen shirt separated those hands from her skin. His mouth ravaged hers, his tongue tasting and teasing. She circled her arms around his neck and held on to him as excitement sliced through her like a well-honed sword, leaving her breathless.

He raised his head, and his eyes smoldered. "You've teased me for days and haunted my very thoughts," he growled, the admission inspiring tingles to spring forth deep inside her. "This once, you will be mine."

She should deny him. He was her prisoner, and she couldn't… All logic faded as his hot tongue delved into her mouth and the scent of wood smoke and man overpowered her senses. His rough whiskers lightly scratching her skin only added to his allure.

His hands at her waist, he flung her onto the bed and followed, prowling up her body on his hands and knees like a predator about to devour his prey. He ran his palm along her hip then grasped a handful of her shirt, tugging it from her breeches. "I long to see your bare flesh," he whispered as his fingers found the exposed skin at her middle.

She reached out to do the same, taking hold of his shirt, but he caught her wrists and raised them over her head, a wicked gleam in his eyes. "I've dreamed of this for days."

A flicker of alarm penetrated her dazed mind. Would he hurt her? Exact his revenge?

Before she could think much more about his intentions, his mouth descended on hers, obliterating all worry. He settled his weight on top of her, his pelvis pressing intimately between her thighs. Her hands held firm by one of his, he lifted her shirt, the bottom edge teasing her skin as he slowly revealed her breasts. Thomas's hungry gaze took her in, and an appreciative smile tilted his lips. He tugged the shirt over her head and tossed it to the floor, then captured a nipple in his mouth. A noise halfway between a groan and a gasp sprang from her throat at the sudden assault, and pleasure shot from her breast to the apex of her thighs.

The desire to restrain her hands apparently all but forgotten, Thomas caressed one breast as he laved attention on the other, leaving her free to touch him at will. She delved her fingers into his blond hair, the texture soft and thick. Each stroke of his tongue generated sparks within her, inflaming a need she'd suppressed for far too long.

She seized his shirt and yanked it from his breeches, but he stopped its progress up his torso, and pinned her with his stare. "Not yet."

"Not yet?" What was he waiting for? She wanted to touch him just as he was touching her, and if he wouldn't let her bare his chest, then... Catherine reached down and laid her hand against his erection, sliding her palm along its length.

His green eyes widened, then gleamed. "Fine. As you wish." He rid himself of the shirt, but her mind had strayed to a new prize. She freed the buttons of his breeches with a desperation she didn't know she possessed. How long it had been since she'd lain with a man, since she'd allowed herself a respite from the harsh realities of life? She'd forgotten how good it felt to be held so intimately. She didn't stop once his erection sprang free. She tugged the breeches lower still.

Thomas did the same, undressing her until they both sat naked on the bed. They studied each other before she pushed him onto his back and kissed him with all the passion she'd kept at bay for six lonely years. He responded in kind, his demands as fervent as her own. His hands aroused and teased until she could stand no more. She reached for his erection, eager to appease the needs she'd suppressed for so long, but once again he stopped her.

"Tell me you want me."

"Isn't it obvious?" she nearly screeched in his ear.

"I want to hear you say it."

Was he mad? "Thomas, let me—"

Clasping her to him, he rolled with her until he lay on top, and the tip of his member grazed over her core. "Say it."

A tremor raced through her, her body begging for release. Why was he making this demand? Because she'd stolen the Ruby Cross from him? Because she'd stolen his pride? *Men.* "I want you," she admitted. *You competitive bastard.*

He plunged home in one sure stroke that pushed all further epithets from her mind. He filled her so completely, she couldn't want for more. She met him thrust for thrust, her hips rocking with his, luxuriating in his weight pressing down on her, his strong arms on either side, his lips grazing her throat.

"Ah, God. You feel so good," he groaned.

She couldn't utter a word. The building pleasure barely allowed her to breathe, much less speak. Instead, she urged him faster with her hands on his backside. Her nails scored his back, and her gasps turned into cries as waves of ecstasy crashed over her. With a hoarse cry of his own, Thomas pulled out and shuddered his release, then collapsed beside her.

Their eyes locked, the passion still burning, but with it a silent admission that they were adversaries. She studied his handsome face, his slightly crooked nose, his tender lips, wishing they'd met under different circumstances. But alas, if wishing did any good, her life would be entirely different.

She smiled and allowed herself to enjoy a moment or two more. "Are you satisfied? Have I made up for all my *teasing*?"

His grin tickled her insides. "Not entirely." He nuzzled her cheek, his lips brushing her ear. "Maybe if we do it again."

Tempting, but… "We probably shouldn't have done it the first time." That said, she smoothed her hand over his prickly cheek, no regrets troubling her.

"Why not? Whom have we hurt?"

No one. That much was true. "You know the deed changes nothing between us." Thomas was still their prisoner. One whom Barnet hated. Dear Lord, if Barnet ever found out about this, he'd be furious. Then what would become of Thomas?

She made a move to rise, but Thomas clasped her waist and pulled her back down. "Don't go yet," he said.

With his arm around her and his warm breath tickling her neck, she almost relented, but the pragmatic voice in her head wouldn't be silenced. He was her captive, and she was a thief. And if given the chance, he would take the cross from her. What's more, there was no doubt in her mind that if the opportunity arose, he would turn her over to the authorities as soon as they reached London. Setting aside his arm, she sat, a sudden sadness eating at her insides. "You should finish your meal. It's getting cold."

Although a flicker of disappointment passed over his features, he nodded and began to dress. "I suppose it's back to the hold with me."

"Afraid so." She retrieved her shirt and pulled it over her head while Thomas finished buttoning his breeches.

"Well, if you have need for another go…" he offered, "you know where to find—"

A knock rattled the door a mere second before it was thrown open. Barnet stood in the doorway, a dark frown on his face and murder in his eyes as he took in the scene in front of him. "Someone thought they heard…" He ground his teeth together, the scar across his lips whitening.

Damn. Her cheeks burned, and she froze in place.

His steely gaze swept over her bare legs, then slid to the mussed bedcovers. "It appears they heard right."

She hurried to don her breeches and belt while the hair at the nape of her neck prickled and rose. The malice in Barnet's eyes… He looked as if he hated the very sight of her.

"Why?" Barnet snarled. "Why him?" He took a step toward her.

Although she held her ground, she had no answer. Well, none that made sense. By all rights, she shouldn't be attracted to Thomas. They had nothing in common and from the first had been enemies rather than allies.

Barnet's face flushed a bright red. "Explain this to me," he shouted, advancing another step, then two.

"Calm yourself, man." Moving swiftly, Thomas placed himself between her and Barnet. A sweet gesture, but Barnet would never hurt her. Would he?

Barnet drew his pistol from his belt and cocked the hammer back, aiming the weapon at Thomas's bare chest. "You! You should have gone to the bottom of the ocean with your ship."

"Wolfrie, no!" The childhood nickname came unbidden, and she cringed when Barnet's glare returned to her.

Thomas eased away from her, his hands held up, watching Barnet's every move. The barrel of Barnet's pistol followed. As did she. "Barnet, put down the gun," she insisted. Thomas wouldn't allow her to get too close. For each step she took toward him, he took another away. Didn't he understand she could protect him? Barnet wouldn't fire with her in the shot's path.

"Why?" Barnet spared her a glance. "You have the cross. You don't need him anymore. Unless you plan to dally with him again."

"No." She hadn't planned to dally with him the first time. It had been a rash, impulsive act. A rather enjoyable rash, impulsive act, but one she wouldn't repeat. Aye, like a drunk in a gin shop, she hadn't thought about the future when she'd made love to Thomas, only about the pleasure to be had. At the memory of the pleasure Thomas had given her, heat rose to her cheeks again, and Barnet uttered a foul oath. He pulled the trigger.

Cursing, Thomas dove to the side, the shot barely missing him, and her heart jumped to her throat. "Enough of this nonsense." She raced toward Barnet, determined to send him on his way. "You'd best leave. Now."

His attention fixed on Thomas, Barnet let out a bellow and barreled forward.

"Stop!" She moved into his path, but he pushed her aside and slammed full force into Thomas, who'd braced himself for the blow.

Thomas grunted as they crashed into a wall, his head bouncing off the wood. Sweet heaven! Barnet clasped a hand around Thomas's throat. She'd never seen Barnet so filled with rage. He attacked as if Thomas were the very devil himself.

Thomas punched Barnet's ribs and belly until Barnet released him, but Barnet recovered quickly and struck

Thomas in the nose and jaw.

Her pulse pounding a frantic beat, Catherine pulled her dagger from her belt and approached them. Thomas staggered from a blow to his chin, but his gaze darted to her. "Stay back," he yelled before he rammed his fist into Barnet's side, doubling him over.

Stay back? But I can help.

Barnet snarled and seized Thomas about the legs, yanking hard. Thomas fell to the floor, and Barnet leaped on top of him, raining blows down on Thomas's chest and head. Thomas attempted to defend himself, but Barnet landed punch after punch. Barnet would kill him!

"Barnet!" Catherine grabbed the ale from the table and splashed him in the face. "Stop! Come to your senses."

Barnet continued his pounding.

She launched herself onto his back, her dagger ready. Before she could threaten him with the weapon, he roared out, half stood, and threw her off. She crashed against the small table, tipping it over, and pain shot through her shoulder as she landed hard on the floor. The contents of the table scattered all around.

"Catherine?" As if the madness she'd just witnessed had vanished like smoke, Barnet raced to her side and kneeled next to her. "Are you injured?"

Biting back a groan, she sat and rubbed her shoulder. "I'm fine." At least they'd stopped fighting.

Thomas made a move to come closer, blood dripping from his nose, and Barnet pulled his knife from its sheath. "This is your fault," Barnet snarled.

She narrowed her eyes and grabbed Barnet's arm. "His fault? That you shoved me?"

"I didn't mean to. He—"

"You had no right to attack him." Catherine rose to her feet, her shoulder still throbbing. "I'm a grown woman, and I make my own decisions."

"No." Barnet's stare sharpened, determination in his eyes. He retrieved the dagger she'd lost during her fall and slipped it into his own sheath. "You, my girl, have been left alone to fend for yerself and Jonas for far too long already. You need a man to lean on, someone more reliable than Peter…" Barnet pointed his knife at Thomas, "or him."

"And that man would be you?"

"Why not me? I've known you just about yer whole life."

"As friends." She'd never thought of him as anything but a friend.

"Only 'cause of Peter." He took her hand in his, his hold tight. "Now we can be more. We can sail the world, you and I."

Her heart spluttered to a halt. "Is that why you agreed to have me as captain on this voyage? To convince me to stay with you?"

"Aye," Barnet admitted. "With you as captain, all knew not to give you trouble, but once I lay claim to you, there'll be no more need for the pretense."

"Lay claim?" The possessiveness of those two words chafed. Living in the warren of St. Giles, she'd had plenty of men who had wanted to *lay claim* to her. She'd fended them off, one by one. "There is no pretense here. The crew voted unanimously. *I* am the captain of this ship. And just because you found me with a man, doesn't mean—"

Barnet's grip became painful. "Marry me, Catherine."

Oh, God. She'd known he had a fondness for her, but

marriage? "I can't." She attempted to yank her hand out of his grasp, but he wouldn't let her go. All the while Thomas watched them with a tenseness to his posture and a muscle ticking in his jaw. "I won't ever marry again," she insisted. Peter had taught her well that the only one she should rely on was herself.

Thomas glanced toward her sword in the corner. *No, he'd be a fool.* Barnet could call reinforcements at any time. Her gaze connected with Thomas's for an instant, and she shook her head in the barest movement before she returned her attention to Barnet. "Besides, you deserve someone who loves you in a romantic way. That's simply not how I feel toward you."

Barnet's lip curled, his glare settling on Thomas. "Because you have feelin's for him."

"I didn't say that."

"You don't have to. You've protected the man ever since he was captured."

"I don't want any more innocent men to die because of me." Enough had been wounded or killed when they'd first attacked.

"What are their lives worth when compared to your son and mother?" Releasing her hand, Barnet stepped toward the window and wedged his blade between the boards at his feet.

"No!" Her breath catching in her throat, she rushed forward. Too late. He snatched the Ruby Cross from its hiding place—a location he'd shown her, insisting the cross would be safe. And it had been, just not from him.

She held out her hand. "Give it to me," she demanded, a chill racing along her flesh.

His stare darkened. "Marry me, and together we will save Jonas and Patience."

That chill turned into heat, fury burning a hole into her chest. "Are you threatening my family?"

He shook his head. "I'm offerin' to help."

"If I marry you."

"Aye."

"If I don't?" she bit out. "What then?" Catherine clenched her fists, the threat to her son too much to bear. "I will hate you forever if my son and mother die because of you."

A movement caught her eye, Thomas going for the sword. The fool. Catherine's heart nearly broke free from her chest as Barnet called out for his men. Two of them entered, and Thomas stopped in his tracks, the sword still well out of his reach.

"Seize him," Barnet ordered, then faced her. "What should we do with him, Catherine? Will he live or die?"

His implication was clear. Thomas's fate depended upon her answer to Barnet's proposal. Marry Barnet and spare Thomas's life? She didn't have to think long to decide. "Don't kill him."

Barnet nodded once and turned to his men. "Take him away. Lock him in the storage room at the end of the hall."

Thomas glanced back at her, concern in his eyes as the crewmen shoved him out the door.

"The storage room?" she asked.

"Our prisoners won't appreciate his bruises and cuts. Why risk an uprisin'?" He cocked his head to the side. "Besides, if you need more convincin', it's convenient to have him close."

All the better to beat him whenever Barnet desired. "If

you want me to marry you, don't hurt him."

A half smile softened his features, although his eyes remained cold and calculating. "If that's what you wish."

"It is." She held out her hand once more. "May I have the cross now?"

He walked to the chest and found a large leather pouch from within, then slid the antiquity inside. He tied the pouch to his belt and gave it a pat. "I'll keep the Ruby Cross safe." Lifting a hand to her cheek, he sighed, his gaze caressing her face. "Don't worry. Given time, I'm sure your feelin's for me will grow."

Highly doubtful. How could she possibly develop feelings for someone who would force her into marriage? She resisted the urge to shove his hand away. He could keep his delusions. At least for the time being. Thomas was safe, and her family would soon be freed. Nothing else mattered today. Still, her stomach churned at the thought of marrying again—especially to Wolfrie Barnet.

Chapter Seven

Thomas stood in the small storage room, his wrists shackled, the chain between them attached to a hook high in the wall. Fettered again. As he had been for most of this trip, only now his nose ached to high hell, much like it had when his brother had broken it all those years ago.

Moonlight streamed through the window, illuminating the crates stacked all around him, supplies stolen from his own ship. Bloody pirates. And yet the theft mattered less at this moment than it once had. All he could think of was Catherine with Barnet, a man clearly besotted with her, but in a way one would call unsound. He'd seen Barnet's like before. Where once the man's feelings might have been pure, they'd since decayed into something darker, an obsession capable of destroying Catherine if given the chance. But what could he do? And why did he care? While she had protected him from Barnet's fury, she'd also been the one to sink his ship and steal his cross…all to save her son and mother. Damn.

The door opened quietly, and Catherine slipped inside the room. Her gaze swept over the crates then landed on him, and his traitorous heart hammered a welcoming beat.

She stepped closer, studying his bare chest and higher to his battered nose and cheek. She settled a gentle hand on his face, her fingers grazing a tender spot. "Has Barnet kept true to his word?"

Thomas shrugged, the chain between his wrists rattling with the movement. "As you can see, I have no more injuries than when last you saw me."

She nodded, relief flashing over her features before the disquiet settled back in.

With a long exhale, he nuzzled his cheek against her palm. "Don't marry him. You'll regret it for the rest of your life."

"I don't have much choice in the matter." Frowning, she pulled her hand away. "Not if you want to live."

She would marry a lunatic for him? He swore beneath his breath. "Why do you feel so strongly about protecting me? I'm no one to you."

Her frown deepened, and a flash of pain glittered in her eyes, almost as if his words had hurt her in some way. Did she have feelings for him? "You're not the only one I'm protecting," she insisted a little too sharply. "Barnet has the Ruby Cross, and no matter what he says, I'm not convinced he'll give it to me unless I marry him. And that cross is the sole means to rescue my family."

Probably true, although she hadn't answered his question—why had she made his safety part of her bargain with Barnet at all? Apparently, she didn't want to say, which was telling in itself. "If you need the cross so badly, then take it from him."

"If only it were that easy."

"I can help you." He would like nothing better than to see the look on Barnet's face when he lost the upper hand.

Her eyebrow quirked. "The two of us against a ship of pirates?"

Hardly. "If we can free my men—"

"We'd still be outmanned. And we have few weapons."

But they could even the odds if they used their wits. "If we executed our revolt when most of the men are sleeping or when we're docking, we could use their inattention to our advantage." His pulse leaped at the idea. Could he convince her?

She shook her head. "Why would I agree to such a reckless plan when Barnet will willingly help me release my son and mother? If I anger him, he might keep the cross for himself."

"I see," he bit out, annoyed by her stubbornness. "You'd rather have your son grow up with Barnet as his stepfather?"

Her gaze hardened. "At least Jonas would be alive."

"Alive, but would he be safe? Barnet is a violent man. He hurt you when you tried to stop him from attacking me."

"He didn't mean to."

Yes, yet it had still happened. "I've seen the way he looks at you, his affection mixed with madness. He can't be trusted. He acts on impulse, using no restraint." No telling what Barnet would do to feed his obsession. In fact... "Barnet sailed with your husband, did he not?"

"Aye. He was his quartermaster the entire time my husband sailed."

"And how did your husband die?"

Catherine's eyes widened, no doubt suspecting what he

might say next. "Don't," she cautioned. After all, it might be harder to marry the man once the truth was known.

He wouldn't be silenced. "It wouldn't surprise me if Barnet killed your husband so he could have you for himself."

She inhaled a sharp breath. "Nonsense." Her attention dropped to the floor as if searching for a way to deny the possibility that his suspicions might be true. "No. You're only saying these things to help yourself, to gain your freedom." She nodded. "Given the nature of your family, I suspect the sole reason you want to help me is to save your pride." Her accusing stare rose to spear him through. "You hate wondering what your family will think when they have to pay a ransom because you were captured by pirates. You, a fancy ship captain."

His hands clenched, her words grating, and yet he couldn't lie. The thought had crossed his mind, but he had other, more pressing reasons for wanting to help her. Although at the moment, with her allegation heavy in the air, he couldn't think of one.

She stepped away, back toward the door. "I should go," she snapped. "Barnet would be furious if he knew I was here."

"Yes, and you wouldn't want to make him furious, or he might do something he'll regret."

Her expression flickered with unease. As it should, since she'd rather rely on a madman than place her trust in him.

. . .

The sun rose steadily over the horizon. Catherine peered at the sight through the wall of windows at the back of her cabin. The captain's cabin. Not that she was much of a captain. Barnet gave far too many orders here.

All night long she'd tossed and turned, thinking about what Thomas had said. Had Barnet been the cause of her husband Peter's death? It couldn't be true. The three of them had been friends since childhood. Inseparable.

She crossed her arms, hugging her middle. Then why did the idea make her stomach feel sickly? What kind of man would she be introducing to her son? Her sweet seven-year-old boy. The memory of Barnet when he'd attacked Thomas last eve sent an icy ripple of dread down her spine. Barnet's actions had been brutal, much like he'd described one of his own father's episodes. His father had been a violent man named Wolfrie who took out his anger on his wife and children…until his son rose up against him, killing him to save their family further abuse. And soon Barnet would be Jonas's stepfather. Good Lord, no. She had to protect her son.

Perhaps… Jonas didn't belong with pirates. Sailing with them would be too dangerous. And what of her mother? Catherine couldn't leave her to fend for herself. Her mother wasn't well. Which meant, she and Barnet would be separated, just as she had been with Peter. He would sail, and she would stay behind with Jonas and her mother. Her life would be the same as it had been these last years. Catherine cringed at the thought. Lonely again and barely surviving. Rubbing a hand over her forehead, she released her breath. She wanted so much more for her son. She rose to her feet and strode toward the door, desperate for fresh air and a wide deck to pace.

On the deck, crewmen were already hard at work,

including Barnet. He stood talking with a sailor not far off. She headed in his direction, although she knew not what she would say. Barnet's gaze darted to her, and he dismissed the man. "Good mornin'."

With a nod, she forced a pleasant smile to her lips. "When will we reach port?"

Barnet tilted his head toward the sky. "If this weather holds, we'll dock in London late tonight."

So soon. She shivered as an image formed in her mind—a minister before her and Barnet at her side. Forcing the vision away, she cursed herself. She should be relieved. Ere long, she'd have Jonas back, alive and well. "Good. As soon as we arrive, I'll contact Simon Brewer to make the trade—the cross for my son and mother."

His eyes warm, Barnet took her hand in his. "Aye, and I'll find a vicar to marry us posthaste." His mouth twitched into a grin, the scar over his lip stretching tight—a scar caused by his father and a belt.

Her pulse took flight, and she pulled her hand away. "The marriage can wait until I have my son."

The warmth in his eyes cooled. "No, we'll be married before."

What? "Why? There's no need to rush."

"No need to rush?" he said with a harsh laugh. "We're pirates. We can't stay in port long or we'll be found out, and I, for one, would rather not hang on Execution Dock." He rested his hands on her shoulders and looked her in the eyes. "Listen well. My men will take the prisoners to a partner of ours who will arrange for their ransoms, while you and I wed, then retrieve Jonas and Patience. After which, we'll return to the safety of the sea."

But Jonas. "My son doesn't belong with pirates."

"We can leave him behind with your mother."

"No." She jerked away from his touch, and pain radiated through her shoulder from the injury she'd sustained last eve by Barnet's own hand. "Jonas stays with me. My mother is frail. They both need me, on land."

"As you wish."

"Truly?" A small sense of relief relaxed some of the tension she'd held.

Barnet nodded. "I'll give up the pirate life and send my men on without me."

Give up the… No. The hairs at the nape of her neck rose one by one. "Who will captain the ship?"

"The crew will elect a new cap'n."

"But…but you've spent six years leading these men…"

His stare dropped to the planks. "In truth, I would have quit long ago if it hadn't been for Peter."

"Peter?"

"We argued about it frequently." He swallowed hard and spared her a glance. "When we started this venture, we thought we'd get rich. At the time, we had no idea what being a pirate was all about, the skill, the cunnin', the ruthlessness required."

"Peter believed you'd eventually succeed, and maybe you will yet." *Please, don't quit.*

"He didn't care if we succeeded or not," Barnet snapped. "Peter never wanted to go back to St. Giles. To him, no matter what happened, this ship was better than the squalor we'd left behind."

An old wound she'd kept long buried split open. She'd always suspected cowardice as the reason Peter never returned to her and their son. Fear of forever living and then dying in a place smelling of piss and stale gin. She felt that fear, too, every day, but she'd never abandon Jonas. Never.

Barnet stepped closer, his voice a scant whisper. "Why did you choose Peter over me?"

The three of them had known one another for as long as she could remember. They'd lived in the same neighborhood, a place better than St. Giles, although not by much. Once the boys had started working in her father's butcher shop, she and Peter had grown closer.

Peter had been fearless and adventurous, always getting them into trouble, and out of it, too. In contrast, Barnet, so meek and quiet, hadn't compared.

Peter had made her feel alive in a world of work-worn faces pinched with exhaustion. He'd excelled at keeping her mind off her worries. Little had they known that once they married, their lives would become bleaker. After several folks had blamed her father's meat for a widespread illness, his shop had closed and their income had dwindled until moving to St. Giles had been their only option. Peter's grand scheme had come to light soon after.

Barnet bent his head, his mouth nearly touching her ear. "Peter never loved you like I do."

With a shudder of revulsion, she stepped back. "Barnet—"

"He spoke badly about you," he added in a rush. "Said all you ever cared about was money."

Over the course of their marriage, they had argued about their lack constantly. A fact she'd regretted for years after he'd left.

Barnet's hands clenched into fists, and he breathed a bit faster. "He grumbled how your mother wasn't worth the food she ate."

A sense of foreboding inspired the hairs on her neck to prickle all the more.

"Peter said he wouldn't be surprised if you whored yourself out, given your eagerness for coin." Barnet's whole body shook, and his eyes glittered with desperation. "I couldn't stand his talk anymore."

Her heart clawed its way into her throat, making it almost impossible to speak. "What did you do?" she rasped.

His gaze shifted away from her, and a chill sank into her skin.

"Barnet, you told me Peter died during a battle at sea. Did you tell me the truth?" She knew the answer even before his hard stare returned to her and he shook his head.

Her breath froze in her lungs. "What happened?"

He turned toward the rail and grasped hold, his knuckles turning white. "We were drunk late at night, and he was sayin' those things, and I… I pushed him overboard."

Dear God. Her legs wobbled for an instant, but she forced herself to stand firm. "Does the crew know?" They wouldn't take kindly to a crewman killing their captain. Maybe if she…

"No, and they never will." His tone held a threatening edge. "Don't be gettin' thoughts like that in your head. Whether you're cap'n or not, they won't believe your word over mine."

Sadly true. He knew these men far better than she ever would. He'd sailed with most for six years. And she had no proof of what he'd done. She glared at his back, the urge to lash out almost too strong to resist. "Why tell me he died in battle?"

Barnet cast her a sideways glance. "We all agreed that a

widow would rather not hear that her husband perished by fallin' overboard while drunk."

Far better than finding out he'd been killed by a friend. "Why confess to me now?"

He faced her once more, his look sincere. "I want no secrets between us, knowin' we'll be married."

Her stomach churned. Married to him? She'd rather die. She itched to slap him and tell him to go to hell, or better yet, run him through with her sword. But the sight of the pouch containing the Ruby Cross stayed her hand. She had no doubt he kept it in plain view on his belt for just such a purpose—a reminder of who was really in control. The quartermaster had become captain.

She'd best keep her wits. She'd let Barnet believe he'd cowed her. The lives of her son and mother depended upon it. And she wouldn't fail them. Not now. Not ever. "I need to be alone," she told him, in the calmest voice she could manage, and marched away from the man she detested, a plan forming in her mind.

• • •

Already morning, judging by the daylight beyond Thomas's small window. Hours had passed since Catherine's last visit. Why hadn't she returned? Why indeed. *Apparently marrying Barnet isn't so distasteful to her after all.*

Thomas cursed under his breath and knocked his head against the wall. His brothers would get a good chuckle out of this one. *A ship's captain for barely a year and he's captured by pirates, his ship sunk, and he's subjected to the indignity of being ransomed to his family.* He yanked at the chain. This time with the fury of a Bedlamite, to no avail.

At least Catherine would have her family back, even if it did mean spending her life with a crazed pirate. The thought annoyed him. He'd offered her a way out of the situation she'd found herself in. Help him and his men escape, and he'd assist her in getting the cross from Barnet. Instead, she'd rather marry Barnet, a man of violence. The sight of her lying on the floor, after the quartermaster had shoved her, still haunted him. She'd be treated to more of the same from her new husband in the coming years. *Damn*.

No wonder she had a ferociously independent streak, considering the men she chose to wed.

The scrape of footsteps near the door gave him pause. The door opened, and Catherine swept into the room, closing it behind her. "You were right. Barnet killed him. He killed my husband!" She paced the area before him, her eyes wild.

Hmm. His guess had proven true. He wasn't sure if he should be impressed with himself or outraged on her behalf.

"And he expects me to marry him, even after his confession."

"Will you?"

"What?" She stopped and glanced at him, confusion clouding her face, as if she'd forgotten he was there, chained to a wall.

"Marry him," he clarified.

She marched a path across the floor again. "No. I won't have my husband's murderer raising my son." Catherine wrung her hands, her pace unrelenting. "I need to think of a plan… First, we'll need…"

He jingled his chain. "A key." Hard to assist when locked inside a storage room.

"Yes. The key to your shackles, but who has it? Do you remember who locked you in here?"

He shook his head. "It doesn't matter. The crewman won't have the key. Barnet will want to make sure you don't release me. He'll have it close at hand."

She frowned, her expression one of annoyance. "Like the cross he keeps in a pouch."

"Exactly." The prize they all wanted.

"It's probably in a pocket." She nodded. "I'll find a way to get it."

"How soon?" No matter when, it wouldn't be soon enough for him.

"Don't worry. We have time. We'll dock in London late tonight, and as you said, we should wait until then to attack."

Was she seriously going to wait that long before releasing him? "Just because I'm no longer chained, doesn't mean we have to attack immediately thereafter."

"But if someone comes to check on you and you're free—"

"I'll detain him."

"And if there are more than one?"

He cast her an incredulous look. She didn't think he could dispatch more than one man at a time?

"Barnet could realize the key is gone."

He cocked his head to the side, his stare mocking. If she were the one chained, she wouldn't be making such excuses.

"Very well," she sighed. "I'll attempt to get the key soon." She rubbed a hand over her face. "Now then, once the crew is busy preparing to dock, you'll release your men, obtain weapons, and attack, while I get the cross."

She'd go it alone? The thought tightened his chest. "How

do you plan to retrieve the cross from Barnet?"

She palmed the hilt of her sword. "By whatever means necessary. I'll fight him if I have to."

Of that, he had no doubt. "But are you prepared to kill for what you want?" Her methods of torture certainly didn't lead to that conclusion.

Despite her show of mettle, worry creased her brow before she raised her chin high. "Perhaps it won't come to that."

"I'm not so sure. Barnet is obsessed with you, and he knows that once you have the cross, you'll have no more need of him. He won't let you go without a fight."

An arrogant smile tilted her lips, her confidence damn attractive...until she spoke. "Are you really so worried about me, or is this your way of telling me you need my help releasing the prisoners?"

Bloody woman. "Absolutely not." He didn't need a woman or anyone else to fight his battles. All he needed was one to unlock these accursed shackles. Good Lord he was tired of being restrained, and this trip had been almost nothing but. "However, my men will need weapons. Which I could obtain if you get me the key."

She flung her hands into the air as if he'd proven some point in her head. "You can't go prowling around the ship. Someone will recognize you. Besides, they likely distributed your men's weapons amongst the pirate crew. Your men will need to make use of what they can find once they're free."

"You're right. Many of the weapons would have been appropriated, but probably not all." It would be worth the look.

Pointing in his direction, she headed for the door. "I'll

see what I can find, but you stay here."

As if he had a choice. Although that wasn't what troubled him most. "Once my men are no longer prisoners, I'll help you get the cross."

She shook her head, her hand on the door handle. "There's no need. I require you and your men to be a distraction, nothing more."

With that, she left the room, her footsteps fading down the corridor. She would be getting a lot more than a distraction if he had any say in the matter. Not only would she likely need his help defeating Barnet, but he wasn't about to let the Ruby Cross leave this ship without him. Catherine could use it to save her son and mother, but that didn't mean he would let their kidnappers keep the relic. It would be his, just as it was meant to be.

Chapter Eight

Catherine strode to Barnet's cabin, her hand on the hilt of the sword hanging at her side. How she wished to slice him through, but if she dared, the crew would have her head.

She and Peter may have had their differences, but Barnet had no right to take matters into his own hands. If Barnet did indeed become her husband and Jonas's stepfather, what would become of her son? Would Barnet see him as a constant reminder of what he'd done to Peter? Would he come to resent Jonas, maybe even wish him gone? Her throat squeezed tight until she could barely breathe. She would keep her son safe from Barnet, no matter what she had to do.

Staring at the door to his cabin, she hesitated before making her presence known. She'd rather not see Barnet's odious mug again, but how else could she get the key? Shoulders back, she rapped on the cabin door, and footsteps approached from the other side. The door swung open, and she faced Barnet.

His eyes widened, and a look of hope softened his features. "Catherine," he breathed. "Come in."

She forced her hand from her sword and did as he asked, stepping into a cabin much smaller than her own. Sparsely furnished, his quarters were orderly and free from clutter of any kind. She cleared her throat. Best get this over and done with. But the words of absolution she'd planned to say wouldn't spring forth. "I can't excuse what you did to Peter," she admitted instead.

Barnet stepped close, his gaze beseeching her to understand. "I did it for you… For us," he insisted. "I will make your life better than it ever was."

She had to stop herself from releasing the bitter laugh that threatened. "How? What sort of job will you find on land? Other than a butcher shop boy, what other respectable job have you ever had?"

"Until I can find somethin' better, I'll go back to work at Eli Harlow's gin shop. He's always in need of men to keep the patrons from beatin' on one another."

Harlow was always in need because his drunken customers would oftentimes take out their troubles on not only one another, but anyone within reach. If he worked there, Barnet might be beaten to bits, which might save her the trouble.

Barnet picked up her hand and laid a kiss on its back. "Catherine, just give us a try."

Inside, she recoiled at his touch even as she curved her lips into what she hoped was a pleasant smile. She'd come here for a reason, and she'd best not lose sight of her goal. "I do appreciate your honesty." At least now she knew how foolish it would be to marry him, the murderous swine.

Now how to get the key? She settled a hand on his chest and gave him her best coquettish look. "This simply feels so strange. We've never so much as kissed." Mentally, she grimaced, the mere thought of kissing him abhorrent.

He drew her closer, grinning. "That is somethin' we can rectify without delay."

Oh God, no. She braced herself.

Barnet dipped his head, his mouth closing in, and she swallowed the rising bile in her throat, one thought foremost in her mind. *Dear Lord, let the key be hidden in his coat pocket rather than in his breeches.*

. . .

Looking about her to make sure she hadn't been followed, Catherine slipped into the storage area, a lamp in one hand and a few items of clothing in the other.

"Where have you been?" Thomas bit out before she could even close the door.

"*Shh.*" She rushed toward him and set down the lamp and garments. "We don't have much time. The crew is preparing to dock."

His green eyes glinted with annoyance. "We agreed you'd free me earlier than this."

Leaning close, she lifted her hands high and winced as her shoulder throbbed. She pushed the ache from her mind and worked to fit the key in the shackle's lock. "We never truly agreed on that point. It really made no sense to me. Why risk discovery?"

His lean jaw hardened, his face so near, their breath intermingled. "Risk discovery," he growled. "You didn't trust me to stay hidden and to handle anyone who might check on me, not that anyone has."

She couldn't quite reach… She adjusted her position, her chest pressing into his, and winced as the pain in her shoulder sharpened. Although he wore no shirt, his body warmed hers from the chilly night air. He bent his head slightly toward her throbbing shoulder as if he might kiss it, but after a moment's pause, drew back. Her gaze slid to his mouth, and she remembered his hot kisses, desire flaring bright inside her. The key clicked home, freeing one of Thomas's wrists. "If it's any consolation, I trust almost no one."

He grunted. In acceptance or disgust, she couldn't rightly tell. And didn't care. He should be grateful she was releasing him. If the key had been in the pocket of Barnet's breeches instead of his coat, she might not be. Thankfully, she was able to make her excuses and leave before Barnet pressed her for more than mere kisses. The other shackle fell away, and she stepped back to retrieve the clothes from the floor. "Here's a shirt, and a scarf to hide your hair. It's the best I could find."

Thomas took the items and pulled the shirt over his head. "No boots?" he grumbled.

"My apologies," she scoffed. "You'll have to make do." She handed him a cutlass from her belt and Barnet's ring of keys.

A red scarf now hiding his golden locks, Thomas glanced her way and tucked the short sword into his belt. "My men will need more weapons."

"There are some stored in a closet on the gun deck, midship, larboard side. The key to the closet is on the ring."

She returned to the door, determination in her steps. "Go. Release your men and provide me with a distraction, then we'll never have to see each other again." A pang of sadness invaded her chest, but she forced the feeling away. Soon this would all be over, and she'd have the cross she needed to save Jonas and her mother.

She grasped hold of the door handle, the metal cool to the touch, and couldn't help herself. She looked at the man she would leave behind and found him staring back.

"Come with me," he said.

"Where?"

"To free my men."

The offer was tempting, if nothing more than to have a few more moments at Thomas's side. What foolishness. A bleak laugh caught in her throat. "I thought you didn't need my help."

"I don't," he admitted, striding forward until he stood by her side. "But if you're with me, I can protect you."

Her spine straightened even as her heart warmed. "I don't need your protection," she insisted, her voice softer than she'd intended it to be. She'd been taught well how to wield a sword. Still, the fierce expression on his face touched a vulnerable place deep inside, and she added, "It's you who will be fighting to escape. I only have Barnet to contend with."

"You're right." A smile flickered on his lips. "Then maybe we should meet afterward and compare our victories."

After all she had put him through—the humiliation of being stripped and bound, the destruction of his ship— why would he want to meet afterward? Unless he desired revenge. Did he want her close in order to turn her over to the authorities and retake possession of the cross? Perhaps. Perhaps not. Either way, she had no intention of giving him the opportunity. "No need to meet afterward. My victory won't be complete until my family is safe." She'd never given him her full name or the exact location of where she lived. Once she left this ship, she should be safe enough from discovery. And to be sure, she would find another place to live, another part of London…another hovel.

She opened the door and scanned the corridor before moving ahead, Thomas trailing behind, her lantern in his hand. They followed the passage, but she raised a hand prior to stepping onto the deck. Although dark, best not emerge together. If Barnet saw them, their plan would fail straightaway.

Catherine moved ahead, and her pulse quickened at the sight of the pier. Many of the crew stood at the rail, eager to be ashore, while others manned their stations as Barnet barked out orders on the main deck. "Ease the helm to starboard."

She kept an eye on Barnet as Thomas passed her and descended the stairs. Her nerves vibrating with tension, she watched Thomas enter a door on the gun deck to gather weapons for his men as planned. A crewman turned as Thomas's back disappeared into the passageway. A questioning look on his face, he followed, motioning for another of the pirate crew to join him.

Worrying her lip, she glanced between Barnet and the doorway the pirates had gone through. Thomas could handle them. He could, and he would… *Bloody hell.* She had time to spare. Trying her best to appear unhurried, she made her way to the door and slipped inside the passageway.

The dread inspired by the ring of steel on steel propelled her forward at a faster pace. Just down the corridor, Thomas fought the pirates with his back to the wall. They each pitted two daggers against his one cutlass.

"You there," she called out. "Stand down."

Thomas's gaze darted toward her, confusion drawing his brows low. Neither pirate heeded her command. "This is Glanville. He's escaped," one yelled. They slashed at Thomas, their blades glimmering in the lamplight. Despite his remarkable skill, Thomas's arm and chest bled from wounds.

She pulled her sword and dagger from her belt and charged ahead. "I said, stand down!" The pirate with crude tattoos covering both of his arms turned to her, clearly perplexed. She knocked one dagger from his hand, and stared at the other. "Drop it," she ordered. Her sword pointing at his throat, he did as she asked while Thomas ran his cutlass through the other. She sent Thomas a hard glare. "You didn't have to kill him."

He shrugged, stepped up behind her prisoner, and knocked him on the back of the head, rendering him unconscious. The pirate collapsed to the ground. "They were trying to kill me," Thomas explained. He dragged the first man into the shadows, then returned for the next, stripping them both of their weapons. "What are you doing here? I thought you were going to stay on deck."

"I was, until I saw these two men following you."

Thomas frowned. "I could have dealt with them myself."

"You're very welcome." She turned on her heel and started for the deck when a hand on her arm stopped her.

"As long as you're here, you can help me carry weapons."

A look of concern softened his features.

Not this again. "I can protect myself."

"I never said you couldn't." He motioned her toward the weapon closet down the corridor. "Not all the crewmen are busy docking the ship. Some are down here. Hide the weapons beneath your coat so we can pass by undetected."

She didn't move. "We agreed we didn't need each other to accomplish our goals." And she'd have to keep a close eye on Barnet to judge when to attack. "I'd best get back on deck."

Thomas held out his hand. "Fine then. Give me your coat."

"No." Without her coat for cover, her shirt offered a view she'd rather not share with a ship full of men. The slight twitch at the corner of his lips suggested he remembered the sight as well. Devious man. He knew she'd refuse to hand it over, giving her little choice but to help him or worry he'd be caught.

He walked to the closet and waved her toward him, arching a brow. "Come now. You'd have me carry them all in plain view, or have my men fight without weapons? They'll be cut down in a matter of minutes."

Very well. She strode forward. "I'll help you free your men, and then we'll part."

"Agreed." He unlocked the closet door and stepped inside. Soon she was weighed down with blades galore, while Thomas had stashed but a few. They found no pistols. Not a surprise. As prized as they were, the crew would have taken every one.

She fairly jingled as she plodded along, her coat bulging at odd angles. Hardly suspicious.

They descended a stairway to a lower deck where

hammocks were strung in a maze of ropes. Voices approached. Thomas doused the light and swept her into the shadows as the glow of another lamp grew near.

"Can't wait to get ashore," a deep voice rasped. "If I'm lucky, I'll get me turn with Alice before the night is out."

"Not if I get to her first," another taunted with a laugh.

The footsteps quickened, too many for just two men, and Thomas drew her into a dark corner, his body blocking hers from view. They faced each other, utterly still and silent, the shadows obscuring their features even from each other. He leaned close, his arms around her, and his chest pressed against hers.

She clasped him tight. Her heart pounding an irregular beat, she held her breath, oddly comforted by Thomas's presence. At this moment, they were allies, despite the past or what might happen in the future.

"The last time I laid with Alice, I came away with a stinkin' itch," a third complained as the men headed up the stairs, and she released the air from her lungs.

"They're gone," Thomas whispered, his breath fanning along her cheek, making her shiver.

It took her a minute to realize she still clutched his sides. "Oh. Yes." She let him go, and he relit the lantern, then once again led the way.

After descending one more flight of stairs, they reached the hold where the prisoners were kept. The ship had two cells, one on each side, both filled to capacity. Metal bars prevented the captives from escaping their cages. Two guards sat at a table, playing a game of cards. They both rose when they saw they had company.

Thomas bent close. "How quickly can you dispatch

yours?" he whispered.

Always a competition. She nearly rolled her eyes. Catherine stepped forward, her coat hanging awkwardly. "Release the prisoners."

"You," one guard said, his face pocked by scars. He pointed a finger at Thomas. "I know you." He pulled a pistol from his belt, but before he could aim it properly, she withdrew her sword and in an abrupt upward stroke, dislodged it from his hand. The other guard, Rupert, a burly man with a constant sneer, surged toward her with a swing of his cutlass. She blocked the blow and prepared for another, the weight of all the weapons strapped to her hips a hindrance she tried to ignore.

While the prisoners cheered for freedom, the poxed pirate drew a blade, his attention still directed toward Thomas. With sure thrusts and parries, Thomas held the man off and sidled closer. In a deft move, Thomas snatched a dagger from her belt. Her breath caught at the swift tug at her hip, but she managed to keep her wits. "Don't distract me," she hissed, dodging a swing of Rupert's sword.

Thomas tossed the blade toward a cell. "My apologies." He crowded in closer, his blade attacking both men.

Blast him. "Stay back. I have this in hand." She nudged him with an elbow, attempting to remain on task.

"So you say," he chuckled, still spreading his blows between the two men, driving them away.

"Stop." Sorely tempted to stomp on his bare toes, she resisted the urge. Clearly now wasn't the time.

As if he hadn't heard her, he pressed his attack until Rupert's spine was nearly against the bars. The hulking pirate grunted, and he tensed before he crumpled to the floor, revealing Thomas's first mate with a bloody dagger in his hand. Thomas finished his battle with a final thrust of his cutlass.

She glared at Thomas, who smiled in response. He'd fought against her. He knew what she was capable of. What right did he have to— The clink of chains rang hollowly throughout the hold. The anchor dropping. "We need to hurry."

Thomas searched the guards for the key to the cells and released his men while she rid herself of the weapons encumbering her, distributing them amongst the freed crew. Her captives' wary looks and confused murmurs didn't stop them from taking what she offered.

Thomas's first mate stopped by his side. He nodded in Catherine's direction. "What's all this?"

"No time to explain," Thomas insisted. "Take a weapon and help the men escape."

Giving her a last questioning look, the first mate accepted the blade she held out to him and joined the rest at the stairs.

"Are you ready?" Thomas asked her as he led her toward his men.

"Yes." The sooner she had the cross back the sooner—

Thomas wrapped an arm around her and hauled her against him, his lips dropping to hers in a kiss so impassioned, excitement jolted through her like a lightning bolt. She couldn't help but kiss him back, her heart in her throat. After this moment, she might never see him again.

He released her much too suddenly, and a cheer arose from his crew. Had he kissed her for their benefit? Damn him. Before she could utter a word, he strode forward, his cutlass held high. "Let's leave this bloody ship!"

With another hearty cheer, they charged up the stairs. She followed, clearing her mind of all but one purpose… reclaiming the Ruby Cross.

By the time she reached the main deck, all hell had broken loose with Thomas's men battling their way to the gangway leading to the pier. She scanned the deck and uttered an oath. Where was Barnet? She searched for him amongst the fighters, the darkness impeding her progress, until she finally caught a glimpse.

A sword in his hand, he cut down one man after another. She raced toward him, her weapons at the ready. "Barnet!"

His head turned at the sound of her voice. "Go to yer cabin. This will be over soon," he called back, blocking a strike aimed at his throat, then slaying his opponent with his next thrust but losing his blade in the process.

He leaned over the body, prepared to pull his blade free, when she approached from behind and laid the tip of her sword to his spine. "Give me the Ruby Cross."

"Catherine." His empty hands held up, Barnet turned about, his demeanor calm as if she were no real threat. "You'll have the cross soon. I only have to get the vicar…"

"No. You'll give it to me now." She brought her dagger to his throat, the pouch containing the cross peeking out from beneath his surcoat. "Hand it to me."

Barnet grabbed her wrist in a firm grip. "I know you. You won't kill me."

Kill an unarmed man. Kill her husband's murderer. The rights and wrongs of it swirled around inside her head. "Perhaps not." She pointed her sword below his waist to an area most men would defend with their lives. "But I have no qualms about cutting off pieces of you if needed."

His nostrils flared, and his lips thinned. The threat of violence in his glare stole her breath. He'd never bestowed such a look on her before. Barnet released her wrist and freed the pouch from his belt. He held it out for her.

Raising the edge of her dagger, she forced him to tilt his head back, then sheathed her sword and seized the pouch from his grasp. Just the feel of its weight in her hand, the knowledge that she possessed the cross once more, soothed the ache in her chest.

She stepped back, eager to be away. A wild look of longing flared in Barnet's eyes and he lashed out, knocking his arm against her wrist so hard her dagger clattered to the planks. She reared away, drawing her sword, but not quickly enough. Barnet gave her a hearty shove, sending her tumbling backward. Her head struck the capstan behind her, and pain blazed through her skull, darkness crowded her vision.

Barnet kneeled at her side. "You'll never be rid of me. I've waited too long to make you mine," he muttered as he reached for her sword.

Spying her dagger an arm's length away, she tightened her grip on the sword's hilt. When he couldn't pull the weapon away at first tug, he cursed. "Release your sword or you will never see your son again."

Barnet's warning burned through her brain, igniting an unquenchable need to put an end to the threats against her family once and for all. She seized her dagger and thrust forward, sinking the blade deep in Barnet's chest.

Shock widened his eyes, and he leaned away, his hand on the dagger's hilt and his shirt growing red with blood. A look of confusion creased his brow as his gaze returned to her. "Catherine, what have you done?"

Her stomach churned, and a tremor raced through her, her pulse frantic.

He fell back, gasping for breath. Shaking, she rose unsteadily to her feet and hurried away, numb to what she'd just done. She veered as far as she could from those who still fought and headed for the gangway. She'd known Barnet for nearly all of her life. Had she killed him? She couldn't help herself. She looked over her shoulder to where Barnet lay still on the deck.

A blade sliced across her arm. She cried out and faced her assailant, a man with one arm—one arm the size of her thigh, holding a blade twice as thick as her own. He eyed the pouch containing the Ruby Cross clutched in her hand. "Give me the cross," he demanded, his cold stare boring into her.

"Never." She held her sword in front of her, her headache growing so intense black spots marred her vision. She blinked and shook her head, but the action made matters worse. She wavered on her feet. Damn.

The sailor swung his sword, and she braced herself, only to be shoved back by a strong hand. Her view became obstructed by a tall form she immediately recognized. Thomas.

In less time than she would have imagined, he turned toward her, her opponent lying in a heap on the deck floor. The shrill, reedy song of a boatswain's whistle reached them from off-ship. Good God. The Royal Navy. Who else would interfere with another ship's matters except the navy?

Others must have had the same thought as a mass of men deserted the ship, pirate and prisoner alike.

Thomas's gaze dropped to her hand and the pouch. "Let's go." He ushered her along with the others. Hiding the pouch beneath her coat, she accepted his assistance, for now, her sword still firmly in her hand. But once she set foot on the pier, she would ward him off before he dragged her to the authorities, reclaimed the cross for himself, and sent her to Newgate.

Her mouth dry as the dust beneath her feet and her head swimming, she hurried down the gangway leading to the pier, Thomas's hand at her back. His first mate met him at its end.

"Round up the men," Thomas told him. She didn't wait for him to finish. She rushed past, but he grabbed her arm. "Catherine, stop."

With the threat of her blade, she forced him to release her, then backed away a few steps, turned tail, and ran. He couldn't have the cross. Her need of it far outweighed his. She panted for air and struggled to run a straight path, her vision ever narrowing until she felt herself crumple. An arm caught her around the waist before she hit the wooden planks of the dock, and the world turned to darkness.

Chapter Nine

From a nearby chair, Thomas studied Catherine in his bed. So pale and still. Too damn still. He leaned forward and set his elbows on his knees. Raking his hand through his hair, he let his head hang. Now nigh upon midday, she'd been unconscious for hours. His gut turned to stone. What if she never awakened? What would happen to her son and mother? What would happen to him? He shouldn't care as much as he did about her welfare or that of her family. And yet, the thought of her never awakening squeezed his heart so tight he could scarce draw a breath. He couldn't lose her. Hell, even if she recovered, the thought of her returning to the Rookery of St. Giles to live…

He lifted his head and stared at her once more—her ebony hair fanning out on the pillow, expressive features that could hide nothing of her thoughts and emotions, and skin so soft he ached to touch its warmth again. *Wake up, Catherine. Please, wake up.*

As if she'd heard him, her eyes fluttered open, and relief flooded him. Confusion wrinkled her brow before she gasped and frantically searched the blankets.

"Looking for this?" Thomas retrieved the Ruby Cross from the table at his side, his attention drawn to it for several seconds. How good it felt to have the cross in his possession.

She attempted to sit, but groaned. A hand to her head, she lay back down.

"Lie still." He set aside the cross and moved to sit on the edge of the bed. Touching her forehead, he checked for fever, as he'd already done, too many times to count. "What happened to you? You have a bump on your head the size of an egg." He grazed his thumb along her cheek. If only he'd been there to protect her.

"Barnet knocked me senseless, is all." She glanced down at her bandaged arm. "Where am I?"

Thomas bit back a growl. Barnet could go to hell. "You're in my house. Safe."

Her dark brown eyes grew wary. "Why am I here?"

"Where else would I take you? You collapsed in my arms." He'd feared she had a mortal injury. To be honest, his wits had left him, and he could think of nothing but bringing her here, to his refuge. He'd summoned a doctor whose silence could be purchased, but the man had done little to tend her. Not a surprise. Blasted doctors.

"What do you plan to do with me?" she asked, a nervous glint in her eyes. "I would have thought…" She rubbed her face with trembling hands. "I'm surprised I didn't wake up in prison."

"I have no wish to see you in Newgate." Hell, Newgate prison was no place for anyone but the utterly depraved.

Even the most debauched areas of London were a luxury in comparison. "Are you hungry? Thirsty?" he asked. "You've been unconscious a long time."

She dropped her hands to the bedcovers and shook her head. "Is that where the crew of the *Sea Sprite* are? In Newgate?" Her eyebrows drew low. "And Barnet... Is he really dead?"

"He is." Thomas's first mate, Hugh, had found out what he could. He'd also gathered their men and notified Gordon Lamont of the fate of his ship. Hugh had definitely earned his wage last eve. "The Royal Navy joined in the fight. They captured several pirates, including Barnet, but he passed away a short time later."

She closed her eyes in a pained grimace, then stared at the ceiling. "I killed him."

"No loss there." Unless... "After all he's done, you don't feel guilt, do you?"

"No, I suppose not."

And yet, her fretful look remained.

"We were friends for such a long time," she admitted. "I still find it hard to believe he killed Peter."

With a dismissive grunt, Thomas cocked his head, incredulous. "He was using the cross, and your son, to force you into marrying him... I promise you, I won't do the same."

Her gaze darted to him. "What do you mean?"

"I want to help you and your family."

She stiffened, and those lustrous eyes of hers clouded with mistrust. "What if I don't want your help?"

"Then you're a fool." Why not accept a hand when it's offered? Instead, she only grew suspicious. Did she really have such a low opinion of him? Or of all people in general?

"You shouldn't go about this alone."

A frown tugged at her lips. "What will you get in return?"

The knowledge that he'd kept her as safe as he could. That he'd reunited a mother and son. He glanced at the cross lying on the table. Not only that. "When it's all done, and you have your boy and mother at your side, I intend to get the cross back."

She turned away to look out the window, but the slight purse of her lips gave away her thoughts. His answer wasn't what she'd hoped to hear. What had she hoped for?

"How will you retake the cross?" she asked.

"I'm not sure yet, but I'll find a way." She needn't worry. He had no intention of involving her. "Now then, who holds your mother and son?"

She peered at the Ruby Cross. If she were in better condition, no doubt she would grab it and run.

He released a long steadying breath. "I could have handed you over to a constable and kept the cross for myself, but I didn't, and I never will. Trust me."

Cathcrine studied him, looking deeply into his eyes.

"I rescued you from a burning ship," he reminded her. "Tried to protect you from Barnet, and saved you from one of your own men last night…and brought you here…"

"Yes, yes. You're right," she conceded, but still gave pause. "Simon Brewer and his men have my mother and son."

"Simon Brewer? The owner of the Brass Lion." A well-known gambling den that catered to the rich.

"He's the one."

"How did you get involved with *him*?" The man had a reputation as a greedy bounder with a penchant for lambasting politicians who didn't act in his favor.

Irritation hardened her jaw for a fleeting moment. "Peter borrowed money from him when he decided to go pirating."

"And the debt was never repaid," he guessed.

"Not in full, no. Peter paid him what he could, but once he died, the payments stopped."

"How much does he still owe?"

She held out her hand. "One Ruby Cross."

When he made no move to give it to her, she muttered beneath her breath and let her hand drop to the bed. "He owes more than I can ever hope to repay."

But why her? "Why didn't Brewer take this up with Barnet and the crew?"

"How?" she scoffed. "Sail after them and demand payment on the open sea? Besides, his arrangement had been with Peter, no one else. Curse his soul."

"But to threaten a widow…" The bastard.

"I'm sure he believed I had contact with the crew and could count on them for help. And he was right." Wincing, she pushed herself up into a sitting position. "Luckily, they hadn't yet left London after telling me of Peter's death."

"And the Ruby Cross?" he asked, propping a pillow behind her, his mind trying to grasp… "How did Brewer even know of it? How did he know it was in my possession?"

She shook her head wearily.

It had probably been his own damn fault. His first attempt at selling the cross had failed. He'd been asking too much, pressing too hard. Had Seacourt defied his wishes and talked to others about the cross? Possibly. Although he'd found another who might have had an interest in buying, that one seemed all too nervous. Had he been warned away?

"Why blackmail you? Why didn't Brewer send his own men to steal the cross?"

"From what I've heard, he tried. His men searched your ship and your home. They found nothing." Her movements slow, she worked her way toward the other side of the bed. "Lord knows, desperation can inspire ingenuity."

The news shouldn't surprise him. He'd known someone had trespassed on the ship. His watchmen had been laid low in the process, but his home? He hadn't noticed anything out of place. How had they broken in? Through a window?

"I don't have time for all this talk, and it doesn't matter. Not anymore." She flipped the covers from her legs. "Now that I'm in London with the cross, I need to go to Brewer and get Jonas and my mother back." She glanced at her bare legs, her brow furrowing. "Where are my clothes?"

She still wore her shirt for modesty. The rest he'd removed for her comfort, and for a good wash. "You're in no condition to be up and about, and even if you were fit to do so, you can't just go charging over there and demand your family."

"I want Jonas back straightaway." On a sharp intake of air, she rose to her feet, so unsteady she could very well fall.

For pity's sake. He rounded the bed and took hold of her arms, forcing her to sit. "I know, but we have to act with our wits about us. Brewer isn't known for his trustworthiness. We have to give him no choice but to hand over his hostages."

"How do we do that?" she asked, leaning into him.

"I can tell you what we don't do. We don't go with the cross in hand into his place of business or his home. He'll be surrounded by his men, and he'll start making demands."

She speared him with a look filled with pain and

impatience. "My son has been in Brewer's clutches for far too long already and my mother... She's ill. God only knows how she's faring."

He took her hands in his. "Listen to me. I know you're frightened for them, and you're eager to get them back now that you have the cross, but if you aren't cautious in how you go about this, all may still be lost."

She nodded. "I understand. Even so, I'm sorely tired of you trying to tell me what to do," she grumbled, although she stayed where she was, snuggled into his side. "I'm my own woman. I've survived in the worst part of London without your guidance or protection for the last six years. I don't need you or anyone else forcing me to follow their lead."

He settled an arm around her, eager to offer what comfort he could. "I'm not trying to force you."

Her face flushed with color. A fine sight to see, considering how pale she'd been moments ago. "Are you sure? You did the same thing on the ship yesterday." She flung her hands in the air. "Come with me to free the prisoners... Take the weapons to my men... And then when we fought the guards, you battled them both rather than let me help."

"Most would thank me for dispatching those men." Not Catherine. For some ungodly reason, she had to do everything herself.

She pulled away from him slightly, her eyes narrowed. "And the kiss, in front of your men, to show all who was the victor—"

"I kissed you to reinforce in their minds whose side you were on. The kiss told them that you are under my protection." He'd done it for her.

Her shoulders relaxed, and she rested against him once

more. "I'm sorry. Perhaps I've been on my own for too long. Now it seems I can't stop myself from questioning the motives behind every helping hand."

Her apology and admission surprised him to no end. In truth, she deserved one as well. "I'm sorry, too. You're right. I have a tendency to take control and become stubborn about doing things my way." Despite his sincerity, the words scraped his throat raw, but he forged on. "I have no doubt that you are more than capable of handling most things on your own. But in this case, it will be difficult, if not impossible, to be rational when you have so much to lose." He could hardly imagine what he'd do in her place. "Let's try to work together, as partners."

"Are you even capable—"

He bent to the side to look her in the eye. Would she really take that tack? She'd just apologized for the same sentiment.

She cringed. "I'm sorry, again. Indeed. Let's work together."

"Good." He settled her back against the pillow and covered her with the bedding. "Rest this afternoon, and we'll go to Brewer's club tonight when there are plenty of witnesses should he decide to do something rash. But the cross stays here, well hidden, so he can't take it from us before you have your son and mother."

"Agreed. Even if we brought the cross along, it would be of no use. Brewer wouldn't hold Jonas and my mother at the club. He's more likely to keep them somewhere no one could chance seeing them."

"My thoughts exactly," he said as he rose to his feet. Hopefully a few hours would be all she needed to recuperate enough for their meeting with Brewer. If he could approach

Brewer himself, he would, but the man would be expecting Catherine, Thomas's partner in this misadventure. Partner. He suspected this arrangement wouldn't be easy for him, or for her. She didn't have faith in anyone, much less him. But what more could he do to earn her trust? Only time would tell.

· · ·

With Thomas beside her, Catherine approached the door to the Brass Lion, anxiety stretching her nerves taut. She wanted her son tonight, immediately, but knew full well that wouldn't happen. *Oh, Jonas. Are you well? I'm getting closer to bringing you home.*

She glanced over at Thomas. He was staring at her again, an admiring glimmer in his green eyes. While at any other time his regard might have inspired excitement, not now. She raised her hands to her hips. "Yes, I'm wearing a dress." His cousin's dress, coat, and hat, the fine quality of which she'd never worn in her entire life. "Look your fill and be done." If she hadn't left her only dress on the ship when they'd fled, she might have worn her own.

He leaned in close. "I can't help myself. You look stunning. Much better than in the shabby suit you've been wearing."

God help her, the excitement did show itself then, shooting from her breasts to her thighs. But alas, it vanished as quickly as it came, and her nerves returned to their quaking.

Thomas knocked on the door. A thickset, savage-looking man opened it a crack. His gaze took them in, the din of the gambling room loud behind him. "No women allowed inside but the ones paid for."

"Mr. Brewer has been waiting for my visit. I have a certain cross he's been searching for." She lifted her chin a notch. "He'll want to see us."

The guard nodded. "Wait here," he ordered gruffly before shutting the door.

"I'll do the negotiating," Thomas insisted. "We go in, set up an exchange time and place, and get out."

He'll what? No. "I beg your pardon. You're not even supposed to be here. This is an arrangement between myself and Simon Brewer," she argued, with more patience than she'd thought she'd have at this moment. "I'm the one who should speak, not you."

He shook his head and heaved a sigh. "Catherine, we've already discussed this. You have too much invested in the result of this meeting. It would be better if I took the lead."

"Yes, I know." Her stomach lurched. Although they had discussed what they'd do when they arrived at the Brass Lion, now that they were here, the need to act on her own was like an itch demanding to be scratched. She couldn't remember the last time she'd allowed herself to rely on another. She smoothed her skirts and inhaled a deep breath. *Thomas will do what is best.*

The door opened, and the guard waved them in. "Follow me."

She stepped into a crowded great room filled with well-dressed men surrounding the several tables that filled the space. The place was elegant, with fine portraits hanging on the walls, barely visible through the fog of pipe smoke. The laughter and voices deafened as the men enjoyed every comfort—food, drink, women, and gambling. So intent on their games, no one took notice of her as she crossed the room to a door in the back, Thomas by her side.

They entered Simon Brewer's office. A desk took up the center of the room, and the man himself sat behind it in a plush chair. In his expensive suit and wig, he looked just as he had when she'd seen him last — fat, smug, and detestable.

"Where is the Ruby Cross?" he demanded. When he spied Thomas follow her through the door, his well-pleased smile faded into a scowl. Good.

"It's in a safe place," she assured him.

The guard who'd led them to the office left, but another stood to Brewer's right, this one with features similar to Brewer's. He had to be the swine's brother.

Brewer pointed toward Thomas. "Why is he here?"

Thomas spoke up. "I have a keen interest in this… *arrangement*."

Brewer's lip curled, and his hard stare landed on her. "I disagree. She was supposed to procure the cross and leave you behind. In which case, she gets her son and I get the Ruby Cross, while you, Mr. Glanville, get nothing."

Dread settled like granite in her stomach. "And mother," she added.

"What?" Brewer snapped.

"I get my son, *and mother*."

He waved her words away, and her heart clambered for her throat. Something was wrong. "Tell me — "

He turned his attention to Thomas. "What do you want?"

"The deal was the cross for *both* my mother and Jonas," she hurled back at him, charging to the edge of his desk. Her hands reached for her sword and dagger and came away empty. Curse this dress. Not that she would have been allowed inside the Brass Lion with weapons strapped at her hips.

Brewer didn't even trouble himself to look her way. "Why are you here?" he asked Thomas.

Her hand clenched at her side, and without thinking, she reared her arm back, ready to plow her fist into the face of the arse sitting before her. Brewer's guard stepped forward when Thomas grabbed her about the waist, hauling her several feet away. *Damn him.*

"I'm here to help her get her family," Thomas answered.

Skepticism rode every line of Brewer's visage. "Why? She planned to steal the cross from you."

"My reasons are my own." Thomas held her tighter when she tried to step away. "Now let's establish a time and place for the exchange."

Brewer turned his attention to her. "Who else knows about our deal?"

A ship full of pirates now likely in Newgate or already hung. "No one."

He rubbed his chin as he contemplated her answer. "Hyde Park, in the thicket just past the Triple Tree. Tomorrow, midnight." He glanced at Thomas, then pierced her with a cold glare. "Come alone."

She pushed away from Thomas, breaking his hold. If his help meant Brewer wouldn't complete the exchange, then Thomas would have no part. "And my mother?" she asked.

"I'll be coming with her," Thomas interjected. "Along with my men."

She shot him an incredulous look. "No, you won't."

Thomas didn't spare her a look. His attention remained squarely on Brewer. "You'll have your men, and I'll have mine, to make certain everything goes as planned."

"Thomas," she warned.

The two men stared at each other as if assessing strengths and weaknesses.

"I have the Ruby Cross," Thomas growled, his stance confident and sure. "We do this my way, or we don't make the exchange at all."

What? She turned to Brewer, prepared to plead her case, but stopped short when Brewer spoke.

"Very well," Brewer ground out. He nodded toward his guard. "See them out, George."

The guard walked toward them and her pulse took flight. "Wait. My mother—"

Brewer pinched the bridge of his nose as if pained. "Your mother is dead."

Her breath left her lungs in a rush, and the world lost its clarity. Dead. Thomas grasped her hand and led her through the gambling room and outside to the street. A shiver ran through her that had nothing to do with the evening chill. As agony bloomed inside her chest, she held onto her anger with both hands.

"You shouldn't have challenged Brewer, making demands," she bit out, jerking her hand out of his and striding forward down the largely deserted street. "I could have lost my son for good!"

Thomas caught up with her, meeting her stride for stride. "I knew what I was doing... The look in Brewer's eyes... He wants the Ruby Cross too badly to let it slip through his fingers." He grasped her arm, forcing her to stop. "He wasn't going to refuse my demands."

She peered at his chest, unable to meet his eyes.

"Demands made because you want the cross for yourself! You don't care about my son! If he were to die…" When she finally looked at him, the sympathy and concern she saw in his gaze cut through her anger and tugged at her heart. "He said he wasn't going to give my mother to me." Her voice cracked, the pain working its way back in. "I was trying to…" She couldn't go on.

Thomas rubbed his hands along her arms. "I suspected he no longer had your mother or that something had happened to her the moment he mentioned he might not give her to us."

He had?

"Why would he keep your mother without asking you to do more of his bidding?"

A sob broke free as memories flooded her mind. Her mother's kind words, her worried face. She'd always been troubled by how much Catherine worked, by how little they had. And now, she was gone. Thomas ushered her into his waiting carriage, then gathered her close and held her, murmuring soothing words as the tears streamed down her cheeks. She cried for her mother, for her son, and for herself, as she hadn't allowed herself to do for as long as she could remember.

Chapter Ten

Thomas poured himself a drink as Catherine sank into a chair in his parlor. He would not soon forget the sight of her tears and misery. Seeing her cry had put an ache in his chest, one that would remain until her son was free. *Damn Brewer.* That bastard needed to suffer for taking the boy away from his mother. Stealing the cross back from him wasn't enough. He swallowed a healthy gulp of brandy, although its usual power to soothe and relax did little for him this day.

"How soon do you need to contact your men to help with the exchange?" Catherine asked in a weary tone. "With your ship gone, will they disperse to different jobs, different ships?"

He swirled the amber liquid in his glass, dreading her reaction to his answer. "They've already been told of my request."

She sat up a bit straighter in her seat. "They have. When?"

Draining the last of his brandy, he inwardly cringed. "I

spoke to my first mate Hugh this morn while you slept."

Catherine's brow drew low, her expression incredulous. "You planned to bring your men to the exchange even before I awoke?" Her hands clamped onto the arms of the chair, and she shook her head. "What gave you the right to make such a decision? This is the rescue of *my* son. What gave you the right to concern yourself at all?"

Was she bloody crazy? "I beg your pardon?" He set down his glass and strode toward her chair. Such a stubborn woman. "You stole the cross from me. I could have taken it back and left you behind. Instead, I'm helping you."

Her chin quavered and she looked away. "Your goals aren't the same as mine. You wish to beat Brewer at a game in which the prize is the Ruby Cross." She swallowed hard and cleared her throat, then stared him in the eyes once more. "Mine is to rescue my son, to have him with me again, safe and sound."

The accusation cut deep, even though an aspect of it was true. Still, her wavering voice cut through his indignation. He kneeled at her side and took her hand in his. "What is wrong with aspiring to achieve both goals?"

She turned her head away, her tears beginning anew. Catherine had been through much this eve. Not only had she learned of her mother's death, but... Well, he could hardly imagine the fear inspired by the demands he'd made of Brewer, the worry Brewer might refuse. "Catherine, my demands on Brewer were in your best interests. If you'd gone alone to hand over the Ruby Cross for your son, what would have stopped Brewer and his men from taking the cross and killing you both?"

Nodding, she wiped the moisture from her cheeks. "I

know." She blinked away all further tears and directed her gaze back at him. "I simply wish we would have discussed the possibility of what you might say to Brewer beforehand."

"I admit, we should have." Perhaps, like her, he had been alone in his decision-making too long. He wasn't used to talking through and potentially defending his reasoning with anyone.

In light of the tremulous smile brightening her tear-stained face, he would indeed consider discussing his plans at length in the future.

"No one should have to suffer the loss of a child as you have. If only we could do more to ensure Brewer never attempts anything like this again." The injustice of it all singed his very skin. "He should have to pay for what he's done... If only we could use the law to our advantage."

Catherine shrugged. "I went to the constables when all this began. They did nothing."

"No surprise there. Brewer most likely has them in his pocket."

Her eyes widened. "What about your brother? Isn't he a solicitor?"

He nodded slowly, the pit of his stomach hardening like a cannonball. "My brother?"

"He works with the courts. He might be able to help us prove our case and send Brewer to Newgate, where he belongs."

Go to his brother Stephen? For help? "We don't need him."

"If we can charge Brewer with the crime of kidnapping," a pained looked flashed over her features, "of killing my mother, you'll easily get the Ruby Cross back and be on your way."

No. He couldn't approach Stephen with this. He wouldn't. He'd never asked his brothers for help before, and he'd rather not start now. "My brother would wonder why I was helping you. Don't you worry I'll tell him about the theft of my cross?"

She stiffened. "Should I?"

"You'd have me lie to my brother, a solicitor?" His argument was weak. Even he could see it for what it was, an excuse. After bragging to his brothers about the Ruby Cross, he could never admit he'd lost it to pirates.

But instead of berating him, Catherine lifted a hand to his cheek, compassion on her face. "Why do you compete with your brothers? Family should be about affection and supporting one another whenever it's needed."

He pulled away from her touch, from her reproach. "Not all families are the same."

"In this, they should be."

Nonsense. He stood, retrieved his empty glass, and headed toward his brandy. "My family strives for success—"

"At the expense of any sort of affinity toward one another." She rose and crossed the room to place her hand over the decanter's top. "Are you truly happy always competing with your brothers?" She rolled her eyes. "With everyone?"

"I'm happy when I win," he grumbled, brushing her hand away and refilling his cup.

"You're impossible."

Why didn't she understand? It was so simple. "I'm the third son. I will never inherit my father's title, his land, nor much of anything else." And his brothers were a great deal older. "For the longest time, when I was small, I had to sit back and watch as my father celebrated my brothers' accomplishments, dreaming of the day his approval would turn in my direction. I have yet to catch up to their count." He took a swallow of his drink, the slight burn and strong flavor welcome. "As you said, Stephen is a solicitor. Any day, he'll become a barrister. And Charles will soon be a bloody member of Parliament. He will also be a baronet with all that comes with the title. While I…" He gulped down the brandy with vigor, until there was nothing left. "I'm just a captain of a ship owned by someone else." He huffed out a breath as he remembered. "Strike that. I *was* the captain of a ship owned by someone else."

Catherine arched a slender brow. "Are you quite through feeling sorry for yourself?"

He cast her a look that should have silenced her. But no, not Catherine. She simply crossed her arms and cocked a shapely hip.

"If we compare lives, your terribly sad story does not come close to what I've endured."

A valid point.

"Therefore, when you're finished with your drunken rant, arrange a visit with your brother, the solicitor, for tomorrow morning. Even if you don't need his help, I do." On those last words, she turned and left, heading toward the bedroom where she'd recuperated most of the day, while he stood in stunned silence.

Grumbling under his breath, Thomas had another drink and prepared himself for the meeting to come.

• • •

Catherine followed Stephen Glanville's butler down a

long corridor, Thomas at her side. She still wore her cape, as Thomas insisted they wouldn't stay long. It appeared he was in a fine bit of temper. Indeed, the frown on his lips hadn't left his face since last night when they'd first spoken of coming here. Unhappy or not, he would survive.

The stately London town house astounded with its eloquent and expensive ornamentation. Had Thomas's brother spent his every pence on frivolous decorations, or was he so wealthy he could waste his excess coin on these fripperies? Yes, she was well aware of the extravagances of the wealthy, but to see it before her very eyes… One of these paintings, one of these vases, could feed her family for God knew how long. Thomas's house didn't have the same wastefulness. Was it because he was rarely there, or because his brothers didn't visit? Or couldn't he afford such luxuries?

The butler announced their presence, and Catherine entered the dining room. The aroma of roasted meats and fresh bread made her mouth water despite having eaten a short time ago. Two men sat at the long table, one reading a newspaper and the other eating his breakfast with a pile of papers resting beside his plate. Both were dressed well, their suits obviously of the finest material. A note of lavender and orange flowers permeated the room, no doubt from the powdered wigs perched upon their heads.

Thomas stepped forward. "Mr. Charles Glanville and Mr. Stephen Glanville, may I introduce you to Mrs. Catherine…" He paused.

She'd never told him her surname. She could lie to protect herself, but she didn't need to. Not anymore. "Fry," she finished for him. "Mrs. Catherine Fry."

Both men rose to their feet and dipped their heads in

greeting, their stares curious.

"What happened to you?" Charles demanded.

By the direction of his brothers' gazes toward Thomas's injured nose, she knew full well of what Charles spoke.

"Nothing to concern yourself with," Thomas replied.

While Charles clearly didn't approve of the answer, Stephen seemed to have no such issue.

"Care to join us?" Stephen asked before sinking back into his chair, his own breakfast half eaten. A late morning meal to start the day? Ah, the life of leisure.

Stephen had a sturdier build than his brothers, his face fuller, and a single blond curl had escaped from his wig. The solicitor. The one they'd come to see.

"Mrs. Fry?" Thomas indicated the food on the sideboard, his countenance tense. Poor man was sacrificing his pride bringing her here.

She gave him a reassuring smile and took a seat. "No, thank you."

Thomas dropped stiffly into the spot beside her, his gaze trained on his oldest brother. "I'm surprised to see you here, Charles."

Charles set aside his newspaper and smirked. "Stephen mentioned you wished to meet with him, and curiosity got the better of me. I had to see what this was all about."

Thomas grimaced, his eyes glittering with annoyance.

Stephen looked up from his papers. "What *is* this all about? You gave no clue in your message. Do you need my help?"

"No." The word was terse and a bit too loud. Thomas cleared his throat. "I don't need your help. I need your knowledge."

Stephen shrugged as if to say those two things were the same, while Charles's lips curled at the edges.

Such children. Catherine spoke up. "He doesn't need your help. I do." Although the men now looked at her, her admission changed nothing. Thomas looked as tense as before. Best get the answers they needed and leave. "My son and mother were kidnapped, and a ransom demanded. And while I have what I need to pay for their return…or rather my son's return." She clenched her hands together beneath the table at the reminder. "My mother died as a captive." She choked on the words, the wound too fresh. "I want Simon Brewer to pay for what he's done. The kidnapping… her death…"

Thomas turned to her, sympathy warming his eyes. "We don't know he killed her. You said she was weak—"

She squeezed her eyes shut. "Even if that were the case… If it hadn't been for Brewer, she could have died at home, surrounded by her family."

Thomas's soft voice drew near. "I'm sorry to say, legally, I don't believe we can prove Brewer caused her death."

"Simon Brewer?" Stephen asked. "Are you sure?"

"Quite," Thomas answered. "We met with him last eve to discuss the exchange. Cath—Mrs. Fry went to the constables, but they've done nothing for her."

Stephen shook his head. "The constables are a worthless lot, easily susceptible to bribes. Besides that, with no proof of murder, he'll be charged with extortion and kidnapping, both misdemeanors. The constables are only required to apprehend those who've committed felonies—"

"If the rumors are true, Brewer *has* committed his fair share of felonies," Charles chimed in. "Although good luck proving any of them."

Catherine couldn't help herself. She needed to know. "What rumors?" What kind of man held her son hostage?

Charles took a sip of his coffee. "I've heard he's held a grudge against members of Parliament for years. Some say he was responsible for the fire that burned down Zachary Moyle's house, and the carriage accident that killed Roger Lyndon's wife."

Arson and murder? "Why?"

"Likely, because of his father," Charles supplied. "Years ago, Simon Brewer's father attempted to sway members of Parliament to improve the conditions of the St. Giles district."

When his pause lengthened, Thomas impatiently prompted, "Go on."

Charles arched an eyebrow as if the rest were obvious. "If you've seen the Rookery of St. Giles lately, it's quite clear he failed."

"Because he was poor?" She vaguely remembered her father talking about Mr. Brewer when she was a girl. A sorry tale.

"I'm sure his poverty didn't help his cause," Charles agreed. "But he was looked down on even more because he was Catholic."

He would have found no friendly faces in Parliament then, much less anywhere else. Even now, no Catholics could hold political office. "What did they do to him that his son is seeking revenge?"

Charles's expression saddened. "Nothing but bully and ridicule him. But it seems that once he realized his breath was being wasted, he turned to drink, drowning himself in the stuff."

"And you want to join the dastardly bunch who drove a poor soul to drink?" Stephen half laughed.

Charles rested his hand on the top of the cane leaning against the table, his fingers closing on its round end. "Not all who serve in Parliament are prejudiced against Catholics."

"Politicians," Stephen scoffed, playfully.

"Solicitors," Charles scoffed back.

Catherine disregarded their banter, concentrating on the problem at hand. How would the knowledge of Brewer's other crimes, even if they were felonies, help them? They had no proof, only speculation and rumor. And his revenge in the name of his Catholic father had nothing to do with his demand for the Ruby Cross...an antiquity of the Knights Templar...an order blessed by the Roman Catholic Church. An odd coincidence. Or was it? "Do you think Brewer's demand of the Ruby Cross has any tie with his crimes against these members of Parliament?"

"If nothing else, I have to applaud Brewer's sense of irony," Charles chuckled. "What poetic justice to use the Ruby Cross of the Knights Templar to destroy his Catholic-loathing enemies."

"On the contrary." A sense of sadness pervaded her heart. "The true irony is that Simon Brewer has the resources his father never had to improve the London rookery they'd called home. But he's chosen to direct his energy toward revenge instead."

"Hold on. The Ruby Cross?" Charles's suspicious gaze bored into her, and she cringed. She should have kept her mouth shut.

"As in *your* infamous Ruby Cross of the Knights Templar?"

Stephen asked Thomas. "The one you're planning to build your shipping empire with?"

Thomas let his head drop for the briefest moment, a foul oath on his breath, before he looked at his brothers once more. "The same," he admitted.

Surprise flashed over both of his brothers' faces, and they exchanged a look.

"Why are you involved in this woman's dealings?" Charles demanded. "With Simon Brewer, no less."

"Who is this woman to you?" Stephen added.

Thomas answered as if their association were of no consequence. "Brewer wants the Ruby Cross in exchange for her son."

"So she's said." Charles leaned back in his chair, studying Thomas with a critical eye. "And you're simply going to hand it over to him? That doesn't sound like you."

"No, I don't plan on just handing it over to him. That's why we're here," Thomas growled. "If I can find a way to get the authorities involved, perhaps to come to the exchange and arrest Brewer for kidnapping, Mrs. Fry can save her son, and I can retrieve the cross," he continued. "Better yet, if we can charge Brewer with his other crimes, we can have him put away for good. In which case, I won't have to worry about further attempts to steal the cross."

Catherine stiffened, her pulse racing. Thomas wouldn't tell them of *her* attempt to steal the Ruby Cross, would he?

"Brewer has been trying to steal it from you?" Stephen asked. "Grand larceny is a felony charge."

Thomas nodded. "Brewer had his men search my home and ship."

"You know this for a fact?" Stephen pressed.

Relief eased her tension. Thomas wouldn't tell them she'd been a pirate. He would stay true to his word. That, and if he told them she'd attacked his ship and taken the cross, he'd have to admit he'd been defeated. By a woman, no less.

Thomas glanced her way. "I have no proof of Brewer's attempt." Only her word, and she hadn't witnessed the acts, just heard of them.

"I see." Charles turned his stare to her. "And how do you know this woman?"

Despite her confidence that Thomas would not give her up, her muscles tightened again.

"How we met doesn't matter," Thomas insisted. "What matters is—"

Charles thrust out a hand in her direction. "How do you know she isn't working with Brewer, using your sympathies to convince you to give Brewer the cross?"

What? She would never…

"She wouldn't do that." Thomas reached over and squeezed her hand. "I've seen her pain over the loss of her mother and son… She speaks the truth." He leaned back, his hand scrubbing his face. "What we have then is kidnapping and extortion…"

"You'll need witnesses at the exchange to prove even that much," Stephen warned.

"True enough," Thomas agreed. "I'll have my crew with me."

Stephen's brow wrinkled. "Are they upstanding men?"

"Most of them," Thomas admitted.

"With anyone but Brewer, it might be enough," Stephen pushed aside his plate, giving them his full attention, "but I suspect along with constables, he has judges in his pocket."

Corrupt law officials and judges? Catherine pursed her

lips. No wonder most people took the law into their own hands. Those expected to protect their fellow man and sentence the corrupt were as crooked as the criminals.

"Then what can we do?" Thomas asked.

Stephen regarded Thomas with all seriousness. "You need a witness so respected that his testimony can't be questioned without raising eyebrows."

Like Thomas's brothers?

Charles, who'd been staring at her for the last two minutes, finally spoke. "Stephen, do you remember the last time Thomas came to us for aid?"

Where had that come from?

"That, too, was over a woman, or rather a girl," Charles said with a laugh.

Thomas's face reddened, and his leg bounced beneath the table. "I didn't come to you for aid."

Stephen chuckled along with Charles. "Seems Thomas likes to surround himself with women who bring him trouble."

"Even if we have acceptable witnesses to prove extortion and kidnapping, those crimes are misdemeanors. We need more," Thomas cut in, his voice sharp. "Which politicians ridiculed Brewer's father? Do you have any idea who Brewer might hold accountable for his father's downfall?"

"Quite a number, or so I've heard," Charles answered, a smile still in place. "Although it's interesting…the leader of the group Brewer finds fault with has remained unscathed."

Thomas leaned forward, his leg now idle. "Who is it?"

"Old Walter Dunn," Charles provided.

Hmm. "Maybe Brewer has been saving his revenge against Mr. Dunn for last," Catherine muttered.

Questioning looks surrounded her, so she put her

thoughts to words. "Imagine what Brewer could do with the money he'll acquire once he sells the Ruby Cross. Such a large sum will give him power, enough power to make Mr. Dunn's life a living hell."

Thomas's brothers cast her disapproving glances at her choice of words. They could disapprove all they wanted. She may be dressed in finery, but she was from the Rookery of St. Giles. And while not exactly proud of the fact, she wouldn't pretend to be of their class.

Thomas didn't seem to notice. "We'll talk to Dunn. Maybe he knows something we can use against Brewer. If he's aware of how Brewer has been exacting his vengeance, he may agree to stand witness and testify on our behalf." Thomas rose from his seat and turned to her. "We should go. We only have until midnight to get things ready."

Get what things ready? It wasn't as if they could build a case against Brewer in these few hours prior to the exchange.

Charles pulled a watch from his pocket and flipped open the lid. "At this time of day, you'll find Dunn at Shergold's Coffeehouse just down the street." He motioned toward the east.

"How do you know this?" Thomas asked as Catherine took to her feet.

As they had when she'd entered the room, the brothers stood. "The old man never changes his habits...or his mind on issues of import," Charles grumbled, returning the watch to his pocket.

"Good." Thomas nodded to them both. "My thanks for your advice," he ground out, then gestured toward the door. "Mrs. Fry."

Thomas ushered her out of the dining room and into

the corridor as if in a great hurry to leave this place. And leave it, they did. Before the butler could even reach the door, Thomas had her outside and on their way.

"What things do we need to get ready prior to midnight?" she asked. He'd already spoken to his men.

"We're going to talk with Walter Dunn."

Now? Then again, he was close by. She rushed to keep up with his long strides. "Visiting your brothers wasn't so bad, was it?"

Thomas's only response was a grunt.

All this nonsense because of pride. "Your brother Charles may have been eager to needle you, but Stephen seemed quite amiable."

"Don't let him fool you. Stephen may not gloat in my face, but I have no doubt, he and Charles are having a good laugh right this minute at my expense."

How dramatic. "All I saw was the usual teasing between siblings. My brother acts much the same." Or he had. She missed his teasing now. "And like brothers should, I think they worry about you."

Thomas's eyes rolled her way.

A laugh bubbled up, but she managed to hold it in. "I could tell," she insisted. "The questions they asked, how adamant they were to know about your involvement... I'm surprised they didn't offer themselves as your respectable witnesses."

"They would never offer. They would insist I ask, maybe even beg," Thomas growled. "And I'm sure Father will hear about this before the day is out."

"Because you could be in danger."

The look he presented her called her the worst kind of

fool. "Because I had to come to Stephen for advice."

Such worry over nothing. "Do you want to know what I think?"

"Not really, but I'm sure you're about to tell me, anyway."

How true. "I think this competition nonsense between you and your brothers is all in your head."

He didn't look her way, but a muscle in his jaw clenched. "You don't say."

"Yes. All this talk of being a third son, and the achievements of your brothers... You've built in your head a rivalry that doesn't need to be there."

He said not a word, just kept walking at a rather quick pace.

She hurried to keep up with his long strides, not finished by far. "Perhaps your father had a hand in your way of thinking. And if that's the case, he should be ashamed."

When he continued to hold his silence, his pace unabated, she grasped his hand and tugged him to a stop. "Simply because you're the third son doesn't make you any less of a man. You don't have to prove yourself to anyone."

"Maybe I have to prove it to myself," he bit out. His eyes flared wide for an instant as if surprised by his own words.

Oh, Thomas. "You prove yourself all the time. When will you be satisfied?"

His eyes met hers with a look of impatience. "I see you're not going to let this rest until you've had your say. So let's have it."

She held in the choice words that came to mind in response to his surly comment. And yet, what had she expected when challenging his beliefs? She took in a deep breath and blew it out before carrying on. "Don't you see?

Your riches, your employment, none of those things truly matter." She rested a hand over his heart. "What matters is who you are in here. You're a good man, Thomas."

His gaze rose to the heavens. He didn't believe her.

Well, he should. She took him by the chin and directed his attention her way. "You said yourself that after you'd taken the Ruby Cross, you could have left me or turned me in to the authorities. Instead, here you are…" She gestured in the direction from which they'd come. "Seeking advice from your brother—although the very thought obviously sickened you—looking for a way to bring Simon Brewer to justice, and helping me get Jonas back, even if it means losing the cross."

He cocked his head to the side, then resumed walking. "I fully intend to take the cross from Brewer as soon as I can."

"I know." Still, he was utterly missing the point. She kept pace with him as he approached the coffeehouse. "Thomas, you are kindhearted, and no matter what has happened between us, you have always been honest with me. Those are the qualities of a good man, not how much money he makes."

He strode to the coffeehouse door. "If you continue, I'm sure to blush."

She heaved a sigh. Whether he believed anything she said, she had no clue. Still, if nothing else, hopefully she'd given him something to think about.

Thomas pulled open the door. They entered, and he reached into his pocket, retrieving two pennies, which he handed to the door attendant. The young man collecting coins for entry and a cup of coffee took one look at her and held up a hand. "No women allowed inside."

"We won't be long." Barely acknowledging the boy, Thomas scanned the long tables. "We're looking for Mr. Walter Dunn."

The attendant's lips pursed. "I insist—"

Thomas stared the poor boy down. "We'll leave all the quicker if you point him out."

The boy's mouth twitched as if he would say something untoward, and he glanced around him, perhaps for someone to step in. No one came. "He's over there." He finally pointed to an elderly gentleman on the nearest bench. "Say your piece and leave."

Thomas nodded to the attendant and flipped him an extra coin.

The single great room was sparsely decorated. Long, rather crude tables lined the floor, their benches filled with all manner of men. From their dress, some were workmen, some sailors, and others were of a higher class. They chatted and read their newspapers as if their difference of station mattered not at all.

They headed to the closest table where Walter Dunn sat wearing a fancy gold brocade suit and an old-fashioned wig, its volume making his head appear twice its size. He spoke with the thin reed of a man in worn attire next to him. "Did you see the hanging last night at the old Triple Tree?" he asked in a guttural voice that raked along her skin.

At his neighbor's shake of his head, Mr. Dunn laughed deep in his belly. "That one was a sight. Gentleman Jack finally met his demise."

Gentleman Jack. She knew the name. Jack Sheppard was a notorious thief who had escaped prison not once, but four times. A hero of sorts to the London poor, and now it appeared he was finally gone.

"Mr. Walter Dunn?" Thomas asked, interrupting the story.

The politician looked up and surveyed them both. "Do I know you?"

"No," Thomas admitted, but charged on, "Do you remember a John Brewer?"

Dunn's brows rose. "What do you want?"

"We have reason to believe his son, Simon, wishes to do you harm," Thomas warned, his voice low so as not to be overheard.

Dunn grabbed the ornate cane by his side and rose. "Excuse me," he told the man he'd been speaking to, then indicated that Thomas follow and headed for the door.

Once outside, the politician stopped and waited. "Go on."

"We've come to understand that Simon Brewer blames you and others for the demise of his father, John," Thomas said.

Dunn tensed. "How do you know this?"

"Rumor mostly," Thomas admitted. "We've also heard that Simon has caused some misfortunes to befall Zachary Moyle and Roger Lyndon. Do you know of these incidents?"

His gaze scanning up and down the street, Walter Dunn gave a slight nod.

Thomas sidled closer. "You must have talked with these men. Is there any proof of Brewer's involvement in these incidents?"

"Why don't you ask them?" Dunn snapped, his hand clenching and unclenching the head of his cane.

"I plan to."

"Then what do you want with me?"

"We have our own situation with Brewer." Thomas

glanced back at her. "He's kidnapped this woman's son, and we need a respectable witness to prove this crime."

What was Thomas doing? Why ask Dunn to act as witness to a misdemeanor? Proving the felonies would be far more important, although not to her. If Brewer was brought to court, she would want him to be held responsible for this crime as well as the others, even if the punishment wouldn't be as severe. Besides, Thomas's brothers would do just as well as witnesses, if only Thomas would ask them.

The politician's eyes narrowed. "Why me?"

"At the moment, you have the most to gain if Brewer is convicted of these crimes. You've been left untouched. You can't possibly believe Brewer has forgotten about you. No doubt, you'll be next."

Dunn eyed a nearby carriage. "I'm sorry. I can't help you."

"But—"

"I have no firm proof of Brewer's misdeeds, and neither do Moyle or Lyndon. If they did, don't you think they would have already brought up charges?" Dunn insisted, taking a step toward the carriage.

Thomas grabbed Dunn's arm before he could get far. "Perhaps I can get Brewer to talk when we complete the exchange for Mrs. Fry's son, get him to admit to his other transgressions."

"No." Dunn scowled and yanked his arm out of Thomas's grip. "Leave me be." He hurried toward the waiting carriage and climbed inside. In a few fleeting moments, he was away.

Thomas raked a hand through his hair. "Why wouldn't he help us?"

"He's afraid… He's seen his associates brought low by

Brewer over the years, and he's just waiting for what will happen to him."

Thomas uttered a curse. "All the more reason to help us put Brewer in prison."

"He doesn't know us, or if he can trust us."

"Then what now?"

What other choice did they have? "We ask your brothers to stand as witnesses."

"No." He marched off, treading the same path from which they'd come.

"Where are we going?" she asked. To speak with Moyle or Lyndon?

"Let's go home. If Dunn spoke the truth, and no one has proof of Brewer's crimes, it's damned unlikely we'll find a politician to act as our witness."

Her stomach clenched tight. If he wouldn't speak to his brothers, then Brewer wouldn't be convicted of any wrongdoing, but at least she would have her son. It would have to be enough.

Chapter Eleven

Thomas led Catherine up the steps to the door of his house, his mind on the woman behind him. Beautiful, strong, courageous. From the first, she'd entered his life like a whirlwind, throwing him off balance. Initially, he'd resented her for her intrusion, but now he was glad to have met her… the pirate who'd attacked, burned, and sunk his ship. He must be losing his mind.

He withdrew his house key from his pocket and heard rapidly approaching footsteps. Two men. The same two he'd seen at Simon Brewer's establishment. Bloody hell. He should have expected this. No time to escape into the house, Thomas went for the blade beneath his coat, but not before the one named George drew a pistol. He waved them inside with the barrel. "Lead the way," he ordered. "We'll be taking the Ruby Cross."

"But my son…" Catherine exclaimed.

He pointed the gun toward her chest. "Inside."

Thomas's protective instincts welled, and he stepped between them. Was the man mad? The idiot would shoot a woman in broad daylight on a street lined with respectable homes? The more muscular brute pulled a blade from his belt. Much quieter form of murder, indeed.

Thomas glanced toward Catherine with an expression that conveyed his intent to act. He hoped she would catch his meaning. She gave an almost imperceptible nod. Good. He opened the door and let her walk through first. He hadn't yet reached her side in the corridor, when she lifted her petticoats and retrieved a dagger strapped to her leg. That flash of sultry skin took him aback, as it did the two men who followed, giving her enough time to strike George across the hand, first with the blade and then with her fist, knocking the pistol away from him. The sudden action left the man stunned.

Thomas seized the second man's wrist before he could lash out with his blade. They struggled for control, the blasted man even stronger than he looked. Behind him, Catherine brought her dagger to George's neck. George grabbed her arm, forced it away from his throat, then shoved her and fled through the door.

Seeing George escape, the brute threw off Thomas's hand and backed away, following his partner's retreat. Catherine rushed to the door after him, and Thomas stopped her from following with an arm about her waist. "You'll get the cross when I get my son," she screamed at the fleeing men, her body shaking in his arms.

"Come away, Catherine." He shut the door and locked it, drawing her into the nearby parlor. "We're safe now."

Despite his words, she clutched her knife as if ready to

battle them again. "Why did they come for the cross? The exchange is tonight." She removed the hat that had become lopsided on her head and tossed it to a nearby table.

"Good question. They must realize we plan to make a case against Brewer." Her back to his chest, he rested his chin on her shoulder and brought her close. "They could have seen us enter and leave my brother's house, then speak with Walter Dunn."

She pulled away and paced the room. "Or the worst has happened." Her voice wavered and tears glistened in her eyes. "What if Jonas is… What if he's…"

"Don't torture yourself with conjecture."

She wrapped her arms around her middle and squeezed tight. "It would make sense. If they have nothing to trade for the cross, they would need to use force."

He stopped her midstride, his hands on her shoulders. "Stop." Grasping her chin, he brought her attention back to him. "It's more likely they want to prevent us from sending Brewer to Newgate." Guilt thickened his throat. He'd made things worse by investigating Brewer. If he'd only let things be, Brewer and his men wouldn't be so eager to silence them. He had no doubt that if he'd handed the cross to those two men just now, they would have killed both him and Catherine.

Her eyes flared wide. "Maybe we can use this attack against them. We can be our own witnesses."

Who would believe them? "It won't work. It would be our word against theirs, and even if a jury ruled in our favor, Brewer could say his men acted without his knowledge. He would remain unscathed."

"Will there still be an exchange?" Catherine's chin

quivered, and her tears fell.

He looked into her eyes with as much conviction as he could muster. "Most certainly. We have the Ruby Cross Brewer wants. There will be an exchange." He hoped to God his words proved true.

She nodded and wiped at her eyes. "The question then is what will happen after the cross has passed hands? Brewer wants us both dead. I'll need to get Jonas away from him quickly."

"I'll have my men with us, all armed and ready."

"So you've said." Confusion crossed her face. "Your crew is so loyal they'll risk their lives for you? For us?"

A half laugh escaped him. "Yes and no. There are some who would defend me to the end, but most will require payment." Therefore, he would pay them all. "They'll get a share of the profits once the Ruby Cross is sold."

"But what about you? You were going to use the proceeds to purchase a new ship."

Indeed, paying his men would cost him dearly, but what else could he do? He shrugged. "I may have enough left when combined with what I've saved. It depends upon the price the cross fetches."

She shook her head, a mixture of gratitude and astonishment playing on her features. "I can't believe you would risk your dream of owning your own ship for me and my son." She settled a hand on his arm, her touch warm and gentle. "Thank you. You're a generous man."

He chuckled as he remembered… "And you're a surprising woman… A blade strapped to your leg?" The way she'd lifted her petticoats, displaying such beauty before extracting something so lethal… Just the memory prompted the most salacious thoughts. Thoughts of stripping away those petticoats for a more leisurely look, and then a touch, a kiss.

"Where I come from, I always carry a weapon. You never know who you might meet on the streets."

He'd almost forgotten the hardships she'd endured, the kind of life she would return to once all this was over. Catherine deserved better. She didn't belong in a hovel, barely able to afford enough food for her and her son. She belonged with him. The thought took him by surprise, then settled into his very bones. He didn't ponder the rights or wrongs of the feeling, didn't worry about what the future would hold, or if the thought were rational or fantasy. Instead, he stared into the loveliest brown eyes he'd ever seen, eyes that shone with kindness, strength, and an unrelenting spirit he admired so much. "You amaze me," he whispered.

A sweet smile curved her lips, and he couldn't help himself. He had to… He lowered his head and kissed her soft, full lips, heaven against his. She responded boldly, her tongue vying with his and her fingers thrusting into his hair. His hands at her waist, he urged her closer and she complied with a throaty groan that inflamed his lust all the more. Eager to divest him of his surcoat, she pushed it over his shoulders, and the garment dropped to the floor. The minx. Her fingers hurried on to the buttons of his waistcoat, releasing them one by one. So this was the way of it then?

She kissed him with a fervor matching his own, as if only he could satisfy her hunger. And he would. Whenever and wherever she desired. Here and now was more than fine. With a quick tug of the ties, he relieved her of her cape and began work on her stomacher and gown. He lavished nibbles on each new inch of skin he bared, although he hadn't bared nearly enough as of yet.

His waistcoat gone, she pulled his shirt from his breeches. "Thomas, please."

Her impatience echoed within him as he tugged away her first petticoat. Dear Lord, why did women wear so many infernal layers? Perhaps he did like her better in her men's garb.

She yanked at the buttons of his breeches, freeing him from their confines. Her hands wrapped around his shaft and he hissed in a breath. His stomach muscles tightened and pleasure shot through his groin. "Ah God, woman, you will be the end of me."

To hell with this. He backed her to the settee and laid her down, hiking up her under-petticoats to feel the woman beneath. Long, lean legs quivering at his touch led to sultry heat and wetness that heightened his need to a fevered pitch. Their lips met once more as her hips tilted toward his hand and soft mewls sprang from her throat.

Out of nowhere, Catherine's eyes rounded and she sat. "Servants," she gasped, her gaze wildly searching the room.

"There are none here," he assured her with a laugh. A fine time to bring up witnesses with them both sprawled half naked on the settee.

"Good. Then come here." She shifted, slipping out from beneath him. Pushing him to his back on the cushioned seat, she positioned herself on top of him, impaling herself on his shaft. His eyes nearly rolled back in his head at the sensations she evoked with the move. He moaned when she repeated the action, lifting herself up and sliding down. Such a beauty. He plucked the pins from her hair, and her tresses spilled around them in a cascade of ebony silk.

His hands roamed over her, but at every angle came against petticoat, stays, or shift. Bloody hell. He pulled her forward in an effort to reach behind her to the strings of her stays.

"Allow me," she purred, resuming her upright position, her hips moving and her chest thrust out as she plucked the ties free, the sight intoxicating.

Quickly she stripped away the stays and tossed them to the floor, her breasts free beneath her shift. His hands moved of their own accord, to feel the weight of that flesh, the softness and fullness.

Catherine's hands roamed, too. They slipped beneath his shirt and over his bare chest. Her eyes closed and her breath came out in pants, her hips pumping faster. Tingling pleasure built in his groin, a growing pressure. He grasped her waist and thrust his hips, plunging deeper, determined to take her over the edge. Her lips parted and she cried out his name, among other delectable sounds. Her body clenched around him in a pulsing rhythm, the sensation too much to take. He barely had time to lift her from him prior to expelling his seed.

He lay back again, Catherine tucked into his side, and their eyes met in a look that held more than just passion. Tenderness too. And trust.

The moment was all too short. In a blink, sadness infused her stare.

"What's the matter?" he asked, feeling her distance herself from him even before she moved.

"Nothing."

Still, she sat and picked up her stays from the floor.

"Catherine, speak to me."

Her hands dropping to her lap, she shook her head. "Nothing can come from this… Whatever this is between us."

"Why not?" He sat beside her and took her hand in his. *I have feelings for you.* Did he love her, or was it simply affection? Either way, he felt compelled to speak, but no words came. A challenge of swords, a competition amongst brothers, hell, facing pirates… All of those he could handle with ease, yet this, baring one's soul, rendered him as weak as a babe.

Catherine tugged her hand from his. "I don't need a man in my life," she muttered as she donned the borrowed stays, struggling to secure the ties in back.

She didn't need a man in her life, or she didn't want one? Her late husband had been a fool to leave her and their son. How it must have hurt her when he'd left to sail the seas. Her pain still lingered. Thomas had seen it in her eyes, in her bearing. What would it take to relieve her pain once and for all? Was he ready for such a task? "I'm nothing like your late husband." Once he committed himself to a woman, he would never leave her to fend for herself.

Her laugh was a choked sound. "Once you have the Ruby Cross, you'll be sailing again."

"Not necessarily," he argued, although he couldn't imagine a life on land.

In a huff, she swung her arm wide. "For a man of wealth, you don't even have servants. Why is that?"

Wealth? "Where did you get the idea that I'm a man of wealth?" He'd certainly never thought so.

She emitted another pained laugh. "You have a great

deal more than I do. More than most people I know," she said. "You could afford servants if you wanted them. Why don't you hire anyone?"

Internally, he grimaced. He grasped her waist and pulled her toward him in order to help her with the damned stays. "Because I'm at sea most of the time."

"Exactly." She shifted away from him until their bodies no longer touched.

"Stay still," he grumbled, jerking the ties tight. "That doesn't mean I can't find employment on land, if I so choose."

She did as he asked, although her diatribe continued. "But that's who you are...a sailor and an adventurer who needs constant challenge." Silence reigned heavy for a moment until she expelled a long breath. "I won't be responsible for keeping you on land. Some day you would resent me for it."

Some day you would leave me because of it? That was really what she thought. "Then come with me."

Her stays secure, she turned and her gaze darted to his. "Do you mean it?"

The idea had come upon him without much thought, but... "Yes, of course I do."

She released a sigh. "Jonas."

The boy would be no problem. "He'll join the crew, become a cabin boy, then learn to sail. Who knows? Perhaps eventually, he can work his way up to captain." The life of a sailor may not be what she'd dreamed of for her son, but it had to be better than going back to St. Giles. What future would the boy have there? "He'll learn a trade that will serve him well his entire life." His heart pounded a bit harder as a thought took hold. If they were to travel together, the three of them, he and Catherine would need to marry. Was he prepared to bind his life with hers forever? And what would she say to the idea? "Catherine, if you come with me…well, we would need to…"

"Let's not talk of it now," she hurried to say, retrieving her petticoat from the discarded heap of clothes. "I need my son back first and time to think."

"Of course." Today wasn't the time for this conversation, for her or for him. She obviously wasn't ready to trust him fully and he… He rubbed a hand over his face. While his tenderness for her was true, the thought of marriage put a sheen of sweat upon his brow. Married. To a spitfire of a woman. A stubborn, willful…pirate, who would challenge and question him every day of his life. A small smile broke free. Perhaps married life wouldn't be so bad after all.

· · ·

Catherine clutched her hands together in her lap as she perched on the settee in Thomas's parlor and glanced again at his clock. Nearly half past eleven. She made a move to rise, ready to pace the room again, her nerves jumping and twitching, but Thomas laid his hand upon hers, stopping her from flight.

She looked over to where he sat beside her so calm, confident, and sure. Although he still dressed the gentleman, she'd chosen to change into her sailing garb for easier access to her weapons. Somehow she'd hoped dressing as a man would also make her feel more powerful, more in control. It didn't.

"You'll have Jonas soon," he assured her.

If only she had half of his certainty. "It's almost time.

Give me the cross."

He didn't stir, although she knew full well he had the antiquity in his pocket, tucked securely in the leather pouch.

"Give it to me," she repeated. "I need the cross in my hand."

He shook his head. "I'll carry it until the exchange."

"But—"

"Brewer will expect me to have it now that I'm involved. So I'll be his target if this is a trap, and we run into an ambush."

"Which would make it safer with me."

His gaze roamed over her face as if memorizing every detail. "Only until they realized I didn't have it, then they'd come after you. I'd rather their attention stay on me. Giving you more opportunity to grab Jonas and retreat."

Once again Thomas was protecting her, but this time she would hold her tongue. Although she'd found it difficult at first, their partnership had become a blessed thing. What a relief to have Thomas to rely on rather than facing Brewer alone.

Facing Brewer. Her breath caught in her throat. What were the odds that Brewer was setting a trap or an ambush as Thomas feared? If that was Brewer's intent, there would be no trade. Was Jonas still alive and well? After all, why had Brewer's men attacked instead of waiting for the Ruby Cross to be handed over just hours later? Her heart clenched. She might never see her son again.

Thomas's hold strengthened, as if he could sense her growing unease. "Tell me about your son."

The image of her little boy flashed inside her head. His light blue eyes always sparkling with mischief, his full cheeks and ready smile. "He's… He's seven years old." Tears blurred her vision, and she blinked them away, her lips curving as she remembered. "Always covered in dirt, always running off." Fondness and pain rode her next breath. "Jonas never stands still, and every time I see him, he has a new hole in his clothes." A typical boy perhaps, and yet every day he amazed her. "No matter if he goes hungry for days or has to help me with the work, he's always been full of cheer. Somehow he manages to be happy under all circumstances, and he has a knack for making all around him happy as well."

The knot in her stomach twisted ever tighter, but she refused to cry. She would be strong, for Jonas. And to do that, she needed to turn her mind to something else. She looked around the room. "Your home is quite different than your brother Stephen's."

Thomas scanned the room himself. "Smaller," he admitted. "Maybe someday…"

"Not only the size. You haven't the clutter of paintings and vases and sculpture." Simply the essentials, nothing more. "Do your brothers never come here?" she guessed.

His lips widened in a sheepish grin. "No, they don't, but I prefer to believe I'm just more practical than they are. I've been saving my money for bigger and better things."

Like a ship. What would it be like sailing with Thomas? Her heart warmed at the thought. Peter had never offered to take her and their son with him. Not that they could have. Jonas didn't belong on a pirate ship. Still, her late husband had never even considered the idea of taking them all away from the daily suffering.

Someone knocked on the front door, and she jumped from her seat. At Thomas's questioning look, she flushed. Apparently, she was a bit on edge.

Thomas stood and crossed to the door. "I've asked my brothers to join us."

Had she heard him correctly? He couldn't have just said… Unbelievable. When Thomas opened the door, both Charles and Stephen stood on the step.

"Thank you for coming," Thomas told them. They nodded in response. Spying her in her men's garments, Charles burst out laughing. Stephen maintained a stoic mien, with the exception of one raised eyebrow.

Thomas had asked them to stand as witnesses? He'd been against the idea when she'd suggested it before. What had changed his mind? It must have been quite a blow to his pride. Although she couldn't tell by looking at him.

He checked the weapons in his belt, concealed by his surcoat, then glanced at the clock. "We'd best be off. My men will meet us at the park." He gestured for his brothers to proceed. They turned about, heading for the carriage that would take them to Hyde Park.

Thomas ushered her out the door and locked up behind them.

"I'm shocked," she couldn't help saying. "You asked your brothers to join us?"

He shrugged and led her toward the carriage. "What choice did I have? Without respectable witnesses to help prosecute Brewer, who's to stop him from taking your son a second time and forcing you to do whatever he wishes? I'm going to try to get him to confess to more than just the kidnapping."

Was that really Thomas's reasoning? Had he requested their presence for her? Proving Brewer's crimes would also ensure the man couldn't go after the cross again or scare off any more potential buyers. Thomas would have no further worries there. No matter his ultimate goal, gratitude welled. They could both benefit from his brothers' help.

He extended his hand to help her into the carriage. "Let's go get your son."

She grabbed hold and climbed inside, praying with all her might that Jonas would be in Hyde Park when they got there.

Chapter Twelve

The carriage came to a stop a fair distance from the park. Thomas was the first to alight, eager to get this matter done. Usually he thrived on a test of skill and wits, but this time all of his calm confidence had fled. He helped Catherine descend from the carriage, wishing he could tell her to go back inside where she would be safe. Alas, not only would she deny his request, but Brewer might not make the trade without her presence. He was the interloper here, not her. Even after her booted feet touched the ground, he kept hold of her hand.

She looked up at him, her tricorn tilting back, and he spied trepidation in her eyes. He could sympathize. The same emotion had set his nerves to twitching. "As soon as you have Jonas, get him and yourself out of here," he ordered, handing her the keys to his house. The fight for the Ruby Cross would likely be a bloody one. "Wait for me there. If all goes well, I'll return shortly."

"I will," she replied.

Good. He had no doubt she would be true to her word. If not for herself, then for her son.

"And you be careful." She squeezed his hand as if willing him to listen. "The cross isn't worth your life."

"Out of the way now," Charles demanded, stepping to the ground beside them. He snapped his watch shut and tucked it back into his pocket. "We've no time to dally."

Indeed. A half dozen of his men waited not far off, those willing to put their lives at risk for a chance at riches. Time to join them. Releasing Catherine's hand, he walked toward his first mate Hugh.

"I'll need the two of you to stay out of sight," Thomas said to his brothers as they all tread forward. "If Brewer sees you, he's likely to grow suspicious and run. Once Catherine has her boy, make sure they get to the carriage and return to my house."

His brothers both nodded, but cast each other looks.

"You will do as I say?" he asked, just to be sure.

"As long as everything goes to plan," Charles agreed.

Fair enough. They reached Hugh, and Thomas gave him a nod. "Once the boy is out of danger, we get the cross." Thomas met the eyes of each man who'd volunteered. "Are you ready?"

A quiet round of *Aye*s surrounded him. "Then let's proceed."

Stephen and Charles separated from the others in order to approach Brewer's men more stealthily, while he and Catherine led his crew directly toward Hyde Park.

They skirted around the open galleries surrounding the Tyburn Triple Tree—sadly, the spectacle of a hanging always drew a crowd. He glanced at Catherine walking at his side.

Pirates were hung at Execution Dock rather than here. Catherine had risked that fate in her quest for the Ruby Cross, for the love of her son. To love that deeply and to be so selfless… He had to admire her for all she'd gone through.

Once past the site of so many deaths, they headed for a nearby thicket of elm trees, where Brewer had said he'd await them. If Brewer were smart, he'd let his men handle this exchange. But any man who would kidnap a child to force a mother to steal knew nothing but selfishness and greed. He wouldn't trust anyone else with the Ruby Cross. He'd want it placed in his own hands.

They stepped beyond the first few trees, the moon casting the barest light into the shadows. Soon figures moved. Brewer's men. By the looks of things, Brewer's numbers were evenly matched with his. Not that it would matter. He had every confidence the skill of Brewer's men would pale in comparison to theirs.

Brewer stepped out from behind a tree, dragging Jonas with him and forcing the boy to stand at his side.

Beside Thomas, Catherine tensed and her footsteps faltered. Thomas would give anything to reach out and soothe her right now. Or better yet, reunite her with her son. *Soon, Catherine. Soon.*

In the dim light, Jonas appeared uninjured, but frightened.

"Mama." The boy lunged forward. Brewer stopped him with a hand clamped onto Jonas's shoulder.

"Jonas." Catherine's voice was a broken rasp so filled with fear his own chest ached.

"Where is the Ruby Cross?" Brewer called out.

"I have it." Thomas withdrew the pouch from his pocket, its weight heavy in his hand.

Brewer watched him closely. "Show it to me."

He opened the drawstring and slid the cross free. Even in the darkness, the jewels in the gold glittered. Beautiful. Enchanting. Thomas's grip tightened, the desire to keep the valuable piece for himself strong.

Although he stood some twenty yards away, Brewer's excitement was visible. "Hand the cross to the woman," Brewer commanded. "She can give it to me."

Indeed she could, but she wouldn't do it alone. Taking a deep breath, Thomas slipped the cross into the pouch and handed it to Catherine. He would have the cross back soon enough. She rushed forward, and Thomas followed, leaving enough distance to put Brewer at ease, but close enough to act if she needed help.

Brewer stretched out his hand, and Catherine shook her head. "I want my son first," she insisted.

Jonas wiggled beneath Brewer's grip, his eyes round. Brewer hesitated, glancing between his men, then lifted his hand from Jonas. The boy raced into his mother's arms, and Catherine hugged him to her as if she'd never let him go again.

"The cross," Brewer demanded.

Her son where he belonged, Catherine tossed the pouch toward Brewer and began to lead Jonas away, her arm wrapped securely around him.

Brewer pulled a pistol from his belt. "Stop," he shouted at Catherine. Damn him.

At the cock of the hammer, she halted, spun about, and shoved her son behind her.

Thomas's heart lurched. Drawing his cutlass, he hurried to her side. "You have what you want. Let her and the boy go."

"Ah, but you're wrong." Brewer smirked. "I don't have everything I want." Brewer's men crowded closer and Thomas used silent signals to better position his crew.

Brewer glared, his eyes as cold as steel. "This might have been a simple trade before you became involved, Glanville. Before you decided to interfere in my affairs."

"This can still be a simple trade." Thomas opened his arms wide in a show of peace. Although, admittedly, he still held a sword in one hand. "You have the cross, and we have the boy, just as you agreed."

"Just as I...?" Brewer shook with his fury. "I *didn't* agree to you poking your nose into dealings that don't concern you."

He lowered his hands. "I don't know what you mean." With the slightest of motions, he waved Catherine back. The closer she could get herself and her son to the edge of the trees where his brothers hid, the better her chance of escape. He didn't look to see if she complied, but somehow he sensed her inch away.

"I've had you watched," Brewer snarled. "You visited your brothers."

He tilted his head and sent Brewer a confused look. "Is that so wrong? I'm not in London as often as I'd like, and family is important to me." At least in some ways. He may not visit his brothers often, but he didn't outright avoid them, either.

"You had a need to introduce Mrs. Fry, a woman from St. Giles, a pirate's widow, to your brothers?" Brewer stared past Thomas's shoulder and nodded.

Dread settled like a stone in Thomas's gut a mere second

before he heard Catherine gasp. He half turned and took a step toward her, then stopped at the sight. One of Brewer's men stood behind her with a knife to her throat.

She pushed Jonas a safe distance away. Hugh caught the boy and dragged him close. He struggled, his small fist landing a solid blow to Hugh's thigh. Hugh stilled him with an arm around his chest. "I'm on your mother's side," he assured Jonas as he surveyed the men around them, watching for an attempt to snatch the boy. Hugh turned in a slow circle, his blade at the ready.

Curse it. This was all his fault. He should have given Catherine the cross to trade for her son and let matters be. Maybe then Brewer would have allowed her and Jonas to simply walk away. Instead, he'd been selfish. His need to regain the Ruby Cross had only placed her in more danger.

"You spoke to Walter Dunn, tried to warn him about me," Brewer snapped. "Tried to get his help."

Sadly, it hadn't done any good. "He already knows what you've been doing to his colleagues."

"Dunn is a dolt," Brewer said with a harsh laugh. "He hopes that if he disregards what's happening around him, he will be spared."

Was that a confession? Not quite. Since he'd already bungled the rescue of Catherine's son, he might as well do what he could to send this devil to Newgate.

"Burning Zachary Moyle's house, the carriage accident that killed Roger Lyndon's wife," Thomas provided. "How many others have met *accidents* caused by your hand?"

The barrel of Brewer's pistol aimed squarely at Thomas's chest. "Aye, I caused those *accidents* and more. All who spat on my father and had a hand in his demise have paid a price, save one."

"Walter Dunn."

Brewer dipped his head. "I've saved him for last. The bastard will soon be living in hell." A wicked smile widened his lips, his glee disturbing. "Destroying Dunn's reputation, poisoning his career—I will enjoy every minute of his descent."

Scanning the scene before him, Brewer's smile faded. "Enough of this." He turned to one of his men, George. "Kill them," he ordered. "Kill them all, but start with him," he said, pointing at Thomas.

George gestured to his men and moved forward, his gun in his hand.

His heart pounded a bit harder. If only he could draw his own pistol without being shot first.

"I think we've heard enough." Charles stepped out of the nearby brush, Stephen beside him. Both of them held firearms.

What were they doing? He'd told them to stay hidden. They wouldn't be able to stand as witnesses if they were dead.

Brewer glared at George, no doubt wondering how he'd let the brothers go unnoticed. Directing the barrel of his weapon toward Charles and Stephen, Brewer backed away, the coward.

His brothers advanced on George from separate directions, drawing the man's attention from Thomas... and Catherine. Dear Lord. Thomas turned around, ready to fight for her. She didn't need his help. Shifting slightly, she rammed her hand onto the hilt of the sword tucked into her belt, knocking the sheathed blade swiftly upward and into her captor's groin. The fellow's mouth dropped open in shock and pain, giving Catherine the leeway to push his knife aside and shove him to the ground. He lay there for a moment, clutching his manhood, moaning.

"Jonas," Catherine called, and her son came running. She pulled him to her side and prepared to fight off any who would stand in her way to freedom.

From the corner of his eye, Thomas spotted someone dashing away. Brewer. Bloody hell. He had the Ruby Cross. Thomas took off after him, but stopped after a few steps and looked back. Catherine battled one of Brewer's men, her son at her side. She could handle herself with her sword better than any man he'd ever seen, with the exception of himself. She would be fine without him. And his crew was still here to help her. No need to worry. No need to stop short of his goal. The Ruby Cross beckoned. He needed to catch Brewer and get the cross or it might be lost to him forever. He needed…

Catherine stood before her son and parried another attack, as his crew and Brewer's men exchanged blows all around her. *Damn it*. Thomas charged into the fray and joined Catherine as a second swordsman attempted to cut her down. Thomas blocked the swing.

She cast him a grateful glance, and all thought of chasing after Brewer vanished. Instead, he and Catherine defended each other's back and watched over her boy. A third opponent joined in and, as if they were of the same mind, he and Catherine fought as one, neither sustaining a nick. Brewer's men soon fell or fled, and Thomas sought out his brothers, his breathing labored.

Standing nearby, they were both alive, although a bit

bruised. Each had used fists and blades rather than their pistols. Wise, considering each gun would have only one shot. Still, they shouldn't have joined the fight at all. "I thought I told you to remain hidden."

Charles shrugged. "It didn't seem like things were going as planned."

"Thought we could help save your hide," Stephen added. "You're welcome."

Thomas hung his head and cursed his own bloody name. They were right. He should be grateful. He looked them each in the eye with the respect they deserved. "Thank you." Catherine had said his brothers cared more about him than a foolish competition. Perhaps she was right, too.

"I've sent one of your crew for the constable," Stephen said. "I'll make sure these men are locked up. As for Brewer, you may want to follow him so we can direct the authorities where to go for the arrest."

Thomas nodded. "I'll take what's left of my crew and go after him." Both to bring him back for an arrest, and for the cross. "You and Charles escort Catherine and her son away from here."

Charles stepped forward, an eagerness giving his features a boyish charm. "You don't want our help with Brewer?"

Stephen's eyes rolled heavenward. "You may go if you wish, Charles. I'll accompany Mrs. Fry. Besides, I have much work to do. Brewer's admission of guilt will help immensely, but the more evidence we can find tying him to these felonies, the stronger our case against him will be."

Charles sent Stephen a look of perplexity. "Simon Brewer ordered his men to kill our brother, as well as Mrs. Fry and her child, and all of Thomas's men."

"Yes. Yes. All will be included in my charges against him. Which only further proves how much there is to be done," Stephen explained.

Charles shook his head. "Solicitors."

"Politicians," Stephen volleyed back with a smile. "Now let's get Mrs. Fry and her son to Thomas's house."

"I don't need an escort," Catherine argued. Her son clinging to her side, she wrapped her arm tightly around the lad.

"Charles, there's no need for you to help me search for Brewer," Thomas insisted. "You've done your part. No need to risk yourselves further, and I leave the decision of an escort up to Catherine." He glanced at the woman in question, his brave girl. "She's quite capable of taking care of herself." To her alone, he added, "Please wait for me in my home. We have much to discuss."

Only after her nod of agreement did he turn away and summon his men. They'd best go if they were to apprehend Brewer before the night was spent.

• • •

Sitting on Thomas's bed, Catherine hugged Jonas to her as she rocked him back and forth. She should be urging her son to rest, but she couldn't let go of him. Not yet. He may have calmed down since the events of tonight, but she had yet to relax one whit. "I'm so sorry," she breathed. If she'd been a better mother, kept a closer eye on her son... She should have protected him from the likes of Brewer and his men.

Jonas allowed her cuddling as he peered at the bedroom, fascinated by the luxury. This room alone was larger than their entire living space. Or rather, their former living space. By now someone else would have snatched up the room they'd left vacant, no matter how pitiful it had been.

"They didn't hurt you, did they?" she asked, almost afraid of the answer, although Jonas looked well.

He pulled away and tugged his shirt past his shoulder. In the light of the candle, the bruise was barely visible, already taking on a yellow hue. "I fought them when they first took me and Grandmother." His gaze fell to her male clothing again, a topic they'd discussed some time ago. "I tried to get away."

"I know," she assured him. "None of this was your fault."

Tears glistened in his light blue eyes. "Grandmother died in her sleep two nights ago." He turned his face away and wiped the tears from his eyes.

She pulled him in close and rubbed his back as her throat grew thick and hot tears stung her eyes. At least her mother hadn't come to a violent end. Of that she could be grateful.

"If I had escaped, maybe Grandmother…" Jonas's voice hitched.

Oh, her poor boy. "No, Jonas. You are not to blame for her death. Don't think in such a way. Your grandmother has always had a weak constitution. It was only a matter of time." For years, she'd worried about when her mother's final day would come. Even with forewarning, the loss was just as painful as when her father had suddenly passed. Tears trickled down her cheeks. Tears of sorrow and relief. She hadn't heard Jonas's voice for nearly two weeks. "I worried about you so much. I'm very glad to have you back."

"Don't cry, Mama," Jonas urged, patting her on the shoulder. "It wasn't so bad."

Her heart aching, she drew in a quavering breath. Not so bad? Her lovely son was trying to cheer her up. She wept all the harder.

"We had a room with two beds," he said with false cheer. "I didn't have to share once. And we had meals, twice a day. Big ones, with meat and cheese."

She gave a shaky laugh and blinked her tears away. "Sounds like you ate better than you ever did at home."

He snuggled in closer. "I missed you."

Her heart nearly broke. "Oh Jonas, I missed you, too."

"Will they come back for me?" Jonas shuddered in her arms, and she thrust her own tattered emotions aside.

"No," she said firmly. "I will never let them get to you again. Never." Her son would be safe now and for always. For her own sanity, she had to believe that, whether true or not.

As for Simon Brewer, Thomas would ensure he'd never trouble anyone again. "I have a…friend who will make sure those men go to jail because of what they've done." Between Thomas and his brothers, Brewer would pay. "In fact, at present we are in my friend Thomas Glanville's house."

Jonas's eyes widened. "He must be rich."

"I don't know about that." Although he certainly had more wealth than they did, and after he regained the Ruby Cross… "Jonas, what would you think about going on a trip?"

"What kind of trip?"

Sailing the seas. It was on the tip of her tongue to tell him, but what if it never came to be? She wouldn't know for sure until Thomas came back. If Thomas came back. Her pulse jumped. She glanced at the door, wishing he would walk through. He'd gone after a ruthless criminal who had murdered for vengeance. What if Thomas… No, he was a capable man, intelligent and highly skilled. He would return.

And when he did, what would happen? He'd never actually asked her to marry him. If he did, would she say yes?

"Never mind. You should get some sleep." She pulled the covers up and tucked him in, kissing him on the forehead. "I love you, Jonas."

"I love you, too, Mama." He closed his eyes, and she lay down next to him, reluctant to leave his side. Her boy, back with her where he belonged.

Tonight, Thomas could have immediately chased after Brewer when he'd seen the cur run away, but he hadn't. He'd fought by her side, protected her son. Thomas was a man of honor. And the way they'd worked together, as if they were of one mind, one heart. What would marriage to a man such as Thomas be like? To have a partner to count on instead of fending for herself. A good father for her son, who could give Jonas a better future. The idea lightened her heart. Life with Thomas. Would it come to be? Somehow it seemed too good to be true. And yet, she hoped and prayed, because deep inside, she knew… She loved him.

Chapter Thirteen

Thomas strode toward the nearest stable, Hugh at his side. Hours had passed since Brewer had run from them with the cross, and still no sign of him. He hadn't been at his club, or at home, and his wife… Brewer's wife knew something of her husband's location, but wouldn't say. Although the glint of anger in her eyes gave Thomas a fair guess. Dread pooled in his stomach at the thought.

If Brewer left London, he would have needed a horse. While this stable might not be the one Brewer typically used, it was the closest, and therefore the fastest way for Brewer to escape. As expected at this time of morning, the stable was still dark as pitch. When they neared the door, an older boy armed with a pistol came into view. He nodded toward them. "Need a horse or carriage?"

"Among other things," Thomas replied.

The boy leaned back and shouted, "Gil! Customer!"

An old man, his gray hair in a queue and his rumpled

clothes covered in hay dust, met them at the door. "How many times…" he rasped out, as if his throat, too, was coated in the dust. He eyed them up and down. "What can I do for you?"

"Did Mr. Simon Brewer take a horse from this stable?" Thomas asked. No sense in beating about the bush. They had no time to waste.

Gil's thick gray brows lowered. "Don't rightly know."

"He would have been here not long before us," Hugh provided. "He's short, potbellied, and carries himself as if he owns the world."

The stableman cocked his head to the side and rubbed his jaw. "*Hmm.* Memory's not as good as it used to be."

So that was the way of it then. "Would a few coins in your hand improve your recollection?" Thomas guessed, already reaching into his pocket.

"Might at that." Gil glanced at the boy, and jerked his head to the side, dismissing his guard. The boy disappeared inside the stable.

Thomas placed a few shillings in the stableman's palm, catching a whiff of his stench—hay and manure. The old coot frowned and jiggled the coins. "Nope, nothin' yet."

Very well. Thomas handed him a couple more.

Gil shook his head. "Still not enough."

Hugh snickered, and Thomas cut him a look that quelled his mirth. "Tell me then, how much did Brewer pay you for your silence?" he demanded.

The old man hesitated before answering. "Twelve shillings."

That much. "Fine." He counted out the coins and paid up. While now he knew Brewer had stopped by, he needed as much information as this man could give. "Did he say where he was headed?"

"He might have," Gil hedged, depositing the shillings into his pocket before holding out his hand again.

Bloody parasite. He tossed him another coin, his last one.

"Mentioned something about Bath, he did."

Headed west then. "Was there anyone with him?"

"Couldn't say."

Like hell he couldn't. This one needed a good neck wringing. Hugh sniffled and huffed, unsuccessfully holding in a laugh. "Have any money?" Thomas growled at him. "I'm fresh out."

Hugh's laughter abated rather abruptly, replaced by a frown as he reached into his own damn pocket and retrieved the necessary coin. He reluctantly handed it over to the stableman, who looked more pleased by the minute.

"He had just one man with him, both in a plenty big hurry," the old man finally answered.

"Did he take a carriage or just a horse?" Hugh demanded, as if somehow he would get more for *his* coin.

Gil wiggled the fingers of his outstretched hand.

"Never mind," Thomas snapped. Although Brewer would want to ride in comfort, a carriage would slow him down. Best assume he was traveling on the back of a horse. "Prepare seven horses," he told the man, then turned to Hugh. "Gather the men. We'll meet back here within the hour."

"You'll need more coin for that," the stableman warned as Thomas walked away.

"I would expect nothing less. You'll be paid when we return." Muttering an oath, Thomas nodded to Hugh and headed for the waiting hired hack.

Behind him, the old stableman wheezed out a laugh. "Any more questions?"

Thomas paid him no further attention. Let him have his fun. All that mattered was tracking down Brewer and bringing the son of a bitch back, with the cross.

He gave the driver his address and climbed into the hack, the carriage lurching with his weight. As he took a seat, visions of his new ship blossomed before his eyes. She would be magnificent, and all his. He'd name her the *Seafarer*, and she would be the first of many vessels under his command.

The carriage rolled forward, back to his house, back to where Catherine and her son awaited him, and a pang of guilt dispersed his visions of glory. Brewer had left his wife behind in his quest to keep the cross. Wasn't he about to do the same with Catherine? Hell no. Brewer was running from the law. He might never return to London. If he did, he would risk discovery and arrest.

Whereas *he* was merely pursuing Brewer in the name of the law, and fully planned to come back to Catherine. In fact, he was doing this in part *for* Catherine and her son, to make Brewer pay for his crimes. To keep them safe from Brewer preying on them again. Besides, now he had men who also had a stake in recovering the Ruby Cross. He owed it to them to lead the chase. Hell, he owed it to himself.

He'd bragged to his father and brothers about the wealth he'd obtain from the sale of the antiquity, about the grand ship he'd buy. One more reason to get the cross back. If his family heard how he'd let it slip from his fingers, oh how they'd laugh. No, he'd find Brewer and the cross, no matter what he had to do or how long it would take. No one could fault him for that.

No one, except perhaps Catherine.

· · ·

Catherine blinked open her eyes. She'd fallen asleep? She'd been waiting on the settee in the parlor with the intent of listening for a knock on the front door, since she'd taken Thomas's key. Now she lay sprawled quite comfortably on the cushions. The floor upstairs creaked. Jonas? She rose from the settee and hurried to her son. The first streaks of dawn streaming through the windows lit her way. Up one flight of steps, she headed to the bedroom and peered inside to find Jonas still asleep in the large bed. Then what had caused the noise?

In the next room, wood slid on wood, like a drawer opening, and her heart leaped for her throat. Retrieving the dagger from her belt, she crept toward the sound. The faint clink of metal reached her as she approached the open door to Thomas's study. "Thomas." She lowered her weapon and blew out a breath. He stood behind his desk, filling a pouch with coins.

He looked at her and smiled. "I didn't want to wake you."

"How did you get in the house? I have your key."

Thomas tightened the pouch string and slipped it into his coat pocket. "I have another."

Of course. She should have guessed.

The satchel sitting on his desk before him was stuffed full, and dread invaded her chest like a ghost from the past. "Are you going somewhere?"

"Yes. Brewer has left London." He uttered a quiet curse.

"The sight of my brothers must have scared him off. He's well aware that we can build a case against him."

"Do you know where he's headed? How long will you be gone?" The words tasted bitter on her tongue. She'd had much the same conversation six years ago, with Peter. Afterward, she'd never seen him again.

"We think he's headed west." He shrugged. "We'll be gone as long as it takes."

Dear God. Not again. His gaze rose to hers, and his brow creased as he studied her face. What he saw there, she couldn't say, but he stepped forward and rested his hands on her shoulders. "I'll be back. I promise."

"When? A day? A week? Perhaps a month or a year?" The bitterness she tasted permeated her tone. She'd been through this before. Promises meant nothing when they hindered a man's dreams. Thomas may seem sincere now, but once away, he would forget. Just as Peter had.

Averting his eyes, he admitted, "I don't know."

She backed away from him. Pain clouded her vision and brought tears to her eyes, tears she refused to shed. What a fool she'd been for allowing herself to dream of a life with him. For allowing another man into her heart.

"You can stay here while I'm gone." He tried to come closer, but she raised her hands and moved away.

"How on earth could I stay in your home without you? If anyone found me here, I'd be accused of trespassing." Who would believe someone of her standing had permission to use this fine house?

Thomas returned to the desk and dug a piece of paper from a drawer. "I could write a note giving you my permission."

He needn't trouble himself. "Then I'll be accused of

forgery, too. Or will you tell our circumstances to someone who can vouch for me? Maybe your brothers."

He stared at the blank parchment lying on his desk as if it would somehow solve the dilemma. "I have no time to explain to them…"

"Who I am to you?" she finished for him. What a conversation that would be. Undoubtedly, his family expected him to marry a proper, wealthy woman who would increase his standing in society, and as competitive as Thomas was, he'd probably planned the same. A woeful laugh threatened, squeezing her throat. She was poor, a thief, a pirate. His family would never accept her.

"We'll settle this when I return." He scribbled words on the page. "In the meantime, stay as long as you wish. If anyone questions you, our family lawyer can attest to the authenticity of my signature."

His signature, whether proven real or not, would make no difference. His family lawyer would reveal her location to Thomas's family, who surely would object to her presence in this home. No, Thomas simply didn't want to discuss the matter, as he was eager to be away. His every movement, filled with energy and haste… He would be out the door as soon as he could.

"Leave. But I won't be here when you return."

"Catherine, don't be ridiculous. Here you'll be safe." He reached into his pocket. "I'll leave you some coin for food and —"

"Stop," she ordered. She'd known what kind of man he was, she'd just forgotten for a time. He was a man of ambition, and she wouldn't stand in his way. What good would it do her to try? "Go after your cross and your dream." She'd survived the loss of one man. She would survive the loss of another.

Thomas nodded, picked up his satchel, and crossed the room to stand in front of her. "I will return." He pulled something from his pocket and pressed it into her hand. His watch. "You'll see." His lips touched hers for the briefest instant before he passed her by, leaving her to stand alone in the study.

He might have meant the watch as proof of his promise, but she knew better. Instead, it served as a reminder of his inner demons, an ambitious nature that would lead to further heartbreak. She set the pocket watch on the desk next to his note, her resolve firm. They would stay as long as Jonas slept, and then they would be on their way.

• • •

Jonas squirmed in his chair beside Catherine as they sat at the kitchen table in the home of Mr. and Mrs. Allen. Their housekeeper, Mrs. Whitworth, was a stern woman as thin as six o'clock, who'd had a frown on her face from the moment she'd let them inside, out of the rain. The woman glanced at Jonas with displeasure.

Forcing a pleasant smile, Catherine rested a hand on his shoulder to still him and looked the housekeeper in the eye. "I was thought well of at my last place of employment. My mistress gave me this dress as a token of her favor." Better to explain her finery before the question came up. She'd hated her continued use of the gown, but what else could she have worn? She'd have to return it to Thomas as soon as she was able. Ah, Thomas. Every time she thought of him, her chest ached. She missed him so very much.

Mrs. Whitworth lowered her gaze, taking in the lace

stomacher of the rose-colored dress, now soaked from long hours walking from house to house. "You were the abigail to Mrs.…?"

"Mrs. Hasting. Yes." Who but a lady's maid would get a mistress's cast-offs? "But I'd be willing to take another position, a housemaid or chambermaid. I could even work in the kitchen," she hurried to add. A lady's maid would likely not be needed.

"You would lower your station? Why did you leave the Hasting's residence?"

"Mr. and Mrs. Hasting moved to France to be closer to their son." The lie slipped from her tongue with ease, as it had countless times this day. "I have no interest in leaving England."

Mrs. Whitworth's eyes narrowed. Had she seen through the lie?

"Do you have a letter of recommendation?" the house-keeper asked.

"No, it was lost when I moved back to London from their country estate." Catherine gave a mental sigh. She wouldn't be hired here. Just as she hadn't been hired anywhere else.

Taking a sip of her tea, Mrs. Whitworth stared at mother and son, making them wait for her assessment. "We do have an open position for a housemaid, but the boy can't stay here."

Catherine leaned forward. This was more progress than she'd had at any other place she'd tried. "He can be an errand boy or help clean pots in the kitchen. He's really very quiet and respectful."

Mrs. Whitworth shook her head. "We have no use for him, but I know a chimney sweep that's always looking for lads."

"No." Catherine stood and took Jonas's hand. She would never sell her boy to one of those men. The chimney sweep was always searching for lads because of how many died in those cramped chimneys—burned or fell to their deaths. Those poor boys. "I'll look elsewhere." She marched toward the servants' door through which they'd come.

"A waste of my time," Mrs. Whitworth grumbled, following them to the door. "Out with you then."

Back into the street, and the rain, they walked on. Dusk would soon be upon them, and she had yet to find a place to stay. Perhaps foolishly, she'd hoped one of these grand houses would take them on, providing both food and shelter. She stifled a hard laugh. Like a twit, she'd let her hopes rise too high. She'd never before worked in a grand home, but she'd prayed someone might hire her. It would have been a great deal better than returning to the dangers of St. Giles. She wanted nothing more than to protect Jonas this time. Her chest tightened. She'd only just gotten him back.

Her usual customers were common working folk who could afford to hire her to wash their clothes or do their mending, but thcy wouldn't offer lodging. Still, she needed employment of some kind.

Jonas tugged on her hand. "Mama, I'm hungry."

"I know, my love. As am I." She had a few coins in her pocket, but first they'd best use what daylight was left to visit a few more potential employers. "We'll find something to eat soon."

He nodded, well used to going without.

They ventured just outside the maze of streets known as the Rookery of St. Giles. A loathsome place, one from which someday her son would escape. Tall two-and-three-story buildings towered in front of them, with the usual congregation of people milling in the foul-smelling street. Drunks and prostitutes mingled with the honest workers returning from their jobs, a great many on their way to the nearest gin shop. They hadn't far to go. Those shops abounded in the Rookery. Her son's hand in hers, she couldn't bring herself to go any farther.

Her breath left her in a long exhale as she spotted a familiar face in the crowd, a neighbor she'd always got on well with. "Anne," she called out and waved a hand.

A slight smile flashed on Anne's lips before her usual tired expression resumed. Anne hurried toward them, a basket of sewing in one hand and a babe cradled to her chest, her fourth child. Thin but sturdy, Anne never complained about her fate, only did what had to be done. "You're back," Anne said when she'd reached them, her eyes widening. "And well-dressed, I might add. Where'd you get the gown?"

"A friend loaned it to me." Her stomach twisted. She'd rather not speak of Thomas. If she did, she might burst into tears. Without him, she felt so hollow inside, like a vital part of her was now missing.

"Must be a good friend indeed." Anne's gaze dropped to Jonas. "Good to see you again, lad."

She blinked away the growing moisture in her eyes. Thomas had been more than a good friend. "I don't suppose my place is still empty," Catherine asked, giving Anne's little boy a smile. While she didn't want to return, they might have no choice.

Anne shook her head. "You know better. The very night you left, someone moved in."

"I had it paid up for the week." Not that it mattered to some. "Know of any place we could stay?"

"'Fraid not. You'll have to ask around, although I don't have to tell you how hard it is to find rooms."

All too true. The Rookery had too few rooms for all who lived there. "Could we stay with you, for a short time?"

Sadness blanketed Anne's features. "I wish you could, but I've taken in my sister and her three. There's barely room to move as is."

Catherine ran a hand down Anne's arm. "I understand." Anne had enough troubles of her own. She didn't need theirs as well. "We'd best be off then."

With a sympathetic look, Anne hurried on her way.

What could she do to secure their future? The St. Giles in the Fields church helped the poor, but she didn't have the necessary certificate of settlement they would require to prove she was a member of their parish. The certificate took time and money, several signatures, and an examination by church officials. As for the workhouse, St. Giles in the Fields had yet to build one, although they planned to within the next year. Still, even if a workhouse were an option, she wouldn't take it. They would separate her from Jonas.

Thomas's house key weighed heavily in her pocket. She shouldn't have kept it. Only God knew why she had, but when the time had come to leave it behind, she just couldn't. All day, the possibility of returning had remained in the back of her mind. Was she being daft, letting her pride stand in the way of accepting Thomas's offer? Even if they were discovered and evicted, what time they could spend in Thomas's house would be far better than returning to St. Giles.

Indeed. What if they returned, for one night, and left again come morning? They could be sly. Never answer the door, stay away from the windows, keep the lights out. Who would know?

"Pard'n me," a deep voice slurred. A slovenly drunkard with sizable girth waved a hand toward them. "Move," he ordered. "I need to piss."

Catherine squeezed Jonas's hand and led him away, her decision made. She headed in the direction of Thomas's house, a mixture of eagerness and dread in each step. While she'd relish the safety his home would provide, she had no doubt leaving in the morning would be no easier than it had been today.

Chapter Fourteen

Damn. Where the bloody hell are you, Brewer? After an entire day of riding, they still had yet to find him. Thomas opened the door to the Culley Inn, one of many such places in the town of Maidenhead. Beyond tired, he located his men just outside the dining room. Hugh and five others. Soaked through from the constant rain, they all appeared as exhausted and dissatisfied as he was. He knew what their answer would be, but asked anyway. "Any news?"

All shook their heads wearily. Blast.

"Don't worry," Hugh assured him, "We know he's here. He'll turn up."

True. They'd followed the trail Brewer had left and had come across two witnesses who'd seen him and another man. He had to be at one of the inns. No doubt he'd bribed the innkeeper to keep silent, but he'd have to leave sometime. "We'll arise well before dawn and wait him out."

The men responded with groans and muttered oaths.

Still, no one objected. Their journey would end once they had Brewer in custody and the cross in hand.

"Let's get something to eat," Hugh suggested. "Then we'll be off to bed and meet again at six."

Thomas nodded. Hugh had the right of it, for the most part. "Go on without me." He'd left his appetite in London. "I'll see you in the morning."

"Are you sure?" Hugh asked. "We haven't had a decent meal since we left London."

"I'm sure. Go on now," Thomas insisted. He turned away and trudged up the stairs to his room, his mind returning to where it had been all day long. To Catherine. Where was she right this minute? Was she safe? He rubbed at the ache in his chest.

Her refusal to wait for him made no sense. With his resources, he could make life so much easier for her and her son. If only she'd trust him.

He entered his room, the accommodations clean and agreeable, the bed beckoning. Heaving a sigh, he locked the door and stripped off his sodden surcoat, then lay down on the mattress, ready for sleep to claim him. But when he closed his eyes, images of Catherine came to the fore. She had such love inside her. He could see it every time she mentioned her son. Of course, it vanished whenever she had spoken of her late husband. Why couldn't she see he was nothing like that man? If given the chance, he would treat her far better. He would love her, protect her, care for her son as if the boy were his own, and always be there for her... Like he was now?

Emitting a growl, Thomas stood and began to pace. He had his reasons for leaving her. Good reasons. He needed the Ruby Cross to buy his ship, to provide for their future. If that wasn't a noble reason… Ah, hell. Perhaps not in her mind. She'd lived without luxuries for the past several years. What he owned already was most likely more than enough to her.

But he'd been striving his whole life to achieve success, and he nearly had it within his grasp. His own ship! His brothers had lives they could be proud of. Why shouldn't he have the same?

Catherine had insisted the competition between him and his brothers was all in his own mind. Was she right in her thinking? His brothers had come to his aid when he'd needed them. Truth be told, they'd put their lives at risk in helping him. They'd never done so before. Although he'd never asked anything of them prior to last eve, either. His brothers had always seemed closer to each other than they'd ever been to him. Now that he thought on it, he might have pushed them away. He'd been so desperate for his father's respect, so in need to prove himself as a worthy son. And for what? Had he ever truly been happy?

For years, he'd been consumed by the desire to make something of himself. From the moment he'd started sailing, he worked hard to climb the ranks in Lamont Shipping. Eventually, he had become his friend James Lamont's first mate, then a captain in his own right. Never once had he stopped and questioned whether his path was one leading to happiness.

Until now. Beautiful, opinionated, and strong-willed, Catherine aggravated him to no end, challenged him at every turn, and made him feel alive. Happy. Fulfilled. Without her, the Ruby Cross meant nothing, just another step forward on a lonely journey that led nowhere. No matter how successful he became, he'd never be satisfied, never be as content as he was with her.

Dear God, what have I done? Thomas retrieved his coat and satchel, and left the room in a rush. He had to find her. He had to make amends. Downstairs, he found his men in the dining room laughing and eating their fill. "Hugh," he called out.

Hugh's attention snapped toward him.

He approached the table. "I'm going back to London."

"Now?" Hugh asked. "What's happened?"

"Nothing... Everything." He rubbed his thumb and finger over his eyes to clear his head. "Nothing concerning you or the cross. It's just something I have to do. If you men go on without me, you'll get an extra share of the profits when we sell the Ruby Cross."

Eyes widened and smiles erupted. *Aye*s resounded from his men. Obviously, they'd miss him dearly.

Hugh's questioning look only strengthened. "This isn't like you, but very well, if you're sure. We'll see you in London as soon as we can."

"Good." Thomas left as quickly as he'd arrived, eager to get on the road. He'd need a fresh horse, then he'd be off, to Catherine.

. . .

Catherine sat behind Thomas's desk, her son asleep in the next room. They'd eaten well from Thomas's larder. Better than it going to waste. Lord knew how long he'd be gone on his quest for the cross. Even so, she would repay him when she could.

She stroked her thumb over the silver pocket watch in her hand. Thomas had left it behind, insisting he would return for her. A promise she'd heard before, and would never believe. He was an ambitious man. He would always want more, want better. And he could certainly do better than her.

Still the pain in her chest wouldn't abate. How had she come to love such an arrogant, domineering, excessively protective man? A man who could be tender and playful. Her heart heavy, she set the watch aside. Best not to think of Thomas.

She should be in bed. The sun would soon rise, and with it, another trying day. She had to find work somewhere, anywhere. Her old jobs? Perhaps. And if not, would a gin shop hire her? Maybe Anne could watch Jonas while she worked serving gin. She cringed at the thought. Jonas didn't belong in St. Giles, a place filled with drunks and whores. She kneaded the heel of her hand into her forehead. What if she sold this gown and paid Thomas back over time? But it wasn't hers to sell. It wasn't even his.

The scrape of boots on the floor caught her attention, and her gaze darted toward the open doorway. Her pulse leaped. Thomas stood there, his hair and clothes dripping, smudges of exhaustion beneath his eyes.

She jumped up from the chair. "Thomas. You've…you've come back."

"Observant, as always," he said with a smile. "I'm surprised to find you here."

Oh, Lord. "Yes, we'll be leaving come morning. I…" Her cheeks burned. "I had difficulty finding a place to stay for the night." Not that she'd looked very hard. Therefore, she'd intruded in his home after she'd firmly told him she wouldn't stay. "I'm sorry. I shouldn't have kept this." She retrieved the key from the desk and stepped forward, holding it out for him.

He made no move to take it from her. "Keep it. I'm glad you're here."

Tears sprang to her eyes, although she had no idea why. Perhaps his kindness was too much. Or perhaps seeing him here, now, when she'd believed she might never lay eyes on him again… The thought gripped her heart and squeezed.

"Besides, you've saved me a lot of time and effort," he added.

"What? How?"

"The entire ride back to London, I wondered how I'd find you again." He glanced toward the window. "At first light, I'd planned to travel all over the city searching for you."

Her breath left her. "You did?"

"Indeed." He took a step closer, and she sidled away, doubt gnawing at her gut.

"You caught Brewer already?" Much quicker than she would have thought. Where would Thomas's ambitions lead him next?

He frowned, his gaze following her every move. "No, my men are still hunting him."

"And the Ruby Cross?" Surely he had it with him.

"Still with Brewer. Catherine…"

"Why did you return?" Had a better opportunity reached him? It would have to be mighty impressive to lure him away from the cross.

He approached and placed his hand on her cheek. "I told you. I came back to look for you."

"For me?" She resisted the urge to nuzzle his palm. This had to be a trick, but she had nothing of value he could want.

His intense stare locked onto hers. "The moment I left here, I couldn't stop thinking about you. About how you wouldn't be here when I returned, and what a fool I was for letting you go."

"Stop." She tore away from him. These were only fanciful words. He might mean them now, but how long before he couldn't resist the itch to pursue his next endeavor, his next adventure? "You don't know what you're saying."

"Catherine, I love you."

The declaration stopped her short. "It won't last."

"Nonsense." Thomas grasped her arms and turned her to face him. "I know your late husband abandoned you. He let his ambitions blind him to what was truly important."

"Are you saying you're not the same? You're every bit as driven to success as he was."

"Not anymore. Not now that I've found what's been missing in my life." He shook his head. "You were right. In all the time I've worked to rise to the status of my brothers, I've never been content. No achievement has ever satisfied me, because happiness is not about money or position, it's about people and enjoying life. I need you. *You* make me happy. Marry me, Catherine."

Her heart stuttered to a halt before picking up its pace once more. Marry him? He'd lost his mind. "You deserve far better than me. Your family will object to a wedding when they find out where I've been living these last six years."

Thomas leaned down, his face inches from hers. "I don't

care what they think. You may not have wealth, but you're my match in every way."

"I was a pirate, who attacked your ship—"

He silenced her with a finger to her lips. "Do you love me?"

"Thomas, I do have feelings for you, but—"

"Even if I never get my own ship, I'm sure I can continue to sail with Lamont Shipping. My offer still stands. You and Jonas can sail with me. He'll learn an occupation that can serve him well."

A laugh bubbled up from the speed at which he spoke, the earnestness in his voice. Peter had done her wrong, but did that mean she had to live alone for the rest of her days? Her heart held the answer.

"Or if you'd rather, I'll change my profession. Stay here with you. I'm sure I can find a suitable job somewhere. Maybe—"

She stood on tiptoe and kissed his lips, her heart full to bursting. His arms came around her and drew her nearer, inspiring that familiar tingling in her middle. He kissed her back with tenderness before pulling away. "Catherine, please tell me what you're thinking."

A smile spread across her lips. "I'm thinking I love you, and I can't wait to be your wife."

He squeezed her tight and lifted her from her feet, then twirled her in a circle, his own grin brighter than the dawning sun.

"Mama?"

Jonas stood in the doorway, rubbing his eyes.

Thomas set her down, and she hurried to her son. "Are you well? Did you have a bad dream?"

Dropping his hands to his sides, he shook his head, his hair sticking up at all angles. "I heard noises coming from in here."

She gestured toward the man walking their way. "Yes, I was talking with Thomas."

"Hello, Jonas. I don't think we've properly met," Thomas said. "My name is Thomas Glanville, and I'd like to ask you a question."

Jonas's eyes grew curious.

"Have you ever wondered what it would be like to sail on a large ship?"

The excitement that lit her son's face warmed her through and through. She turned her attention to the one who inspired the look, the amazing man whom she'd soon call husband. In the time she'd known him, he'd challenged her to her limits, defended her, and protected her. Now he was giving her a second chance at life. As a pirate, she may have robbed him of the Ruby Cross, but Thomas was the one who'd stolen her heart. And she couldn't be happier about it.

Epilogue

The church bells ringing, Catherine kept Jonas's hand in hers as she walked to the small chapel, her palms clammy despite the chilly December air. The pale blue gown Thomas had purchased for her was the best she'd ever owned, its lace and ribbons delicate and pretty, and the fine cloak she wore kept her perfectly warm. She clutched the small bouquet of roses, sweet peas, and rosemary. The garland in her hair of the same flowers and herbs rested heavily on her head.

The sun high in the sky, the few guests they'd invited flocked to the church, nodding as they passed, and her pulse fluttered. Was this a mistake, as her last marriage had been? She looked down at her son. Her last marriage might have been a mistake, but the best thing to ever happen to her had come out of it. Jonas. Her boy.

"Are you sure you have no issue with me getting married? With us sailing away?" she asked him.

Jonas's brow furrowed. "I like Thomas."

Of that she had no question. "So do I."

"Then let's go." He tugged her forward, urging her to move faster.

Ah, the reasoning of a child, so forthright and trusting. She did love Thomas with her heart and soul, but was it enough?

They stepped inside the chapel, and her gaze flew to her groom waiting in the front of the church, handsomely dressed in a gray silk suit. He locked eyes with her and smiled. She tingled all over in response, and her breath caught. She detected not a glimmer of doubt in his stare. He stood tall and confident, an alluring sight she couldn't resist. She dispensed of her cloak and strode down the aisle, all of their guests, what few there were, watching from the pews. With Jonas by her side, she met Thomas and the minister, her remaining doubts fading. Thomas was her love, her life, and her future. Come what may, she would never regret marrying him.

"Dearly beloved friends, we are gathered together here in the sight of God, and in the face of his congregation, to join together this man and this woman in holy matrimony…"

As the minister spoke, she admired the man beside her. How fortunate she was to have met him. Any other man would have grown to hate her for her acts of piracy. Not Thomas. He'd not only forgiven her, but saved her son, and promised her a future filled with love and adventure.

"Therefore if any man can show any just cause, why they may not lawfully be joined together let him now speak, or else hereafter forever hold his peace."

Silence followed the minister's request, as she knew it would. Thomas's brothers hadn't objected to the union.

Neither had his mother or father. Indeed, his father's only reply had been to congratulate Thomas on being the first of the brothers to find a wife.

The ceremony continued, and soon their vows were said and Thomas slipped a gold band on her finger, his voice soft yet steadfast as he declared, "With this ring I thee wed; with my body I thee worship, and with all my worldly goods I thee endow." The manner in which he said those words, as if he spoke to her alone, bound her to him more than a simple vow ever could. Their fingers entwined, she gazed into his warm green eyes, truly happy.

"…I pronounce that they be man and wife together. In the name of the father, the son, and the Holy Ghost. Amen."

A cheer arose, but she barely noticed their audience as Thomas bent his head and settled his lips on hers. Their first kiss as man and wife. She could scarce believe her good fortune.

Within minutes, all those who attended the ceremony left the church, the bells pealing loudly again. Thomas offered his arm. "Mrs. Glanville," he said with a wide grin.

"Thank you, Mr. Glanville." She took his arm, and she, Thomas, and Jonas followed the crowd, stopping for her cloak along the way. Once outside, the cheering began anew and grains of wheat were flung in her direction. Wheat for fertility. Ah, yes, she'd forgotten that part.

Jonas wandered away to inspect a stone that had worked its way loose in the street. She kept him in her sight as Thomas's brothers approached.

Charles nodded. "Congratulations to you both."

"Yes, congratulations," Stephen agreed.

"Thank you," she and Thomas responded at exactly the

same time, eliciting smiles from both brothers.

"And thank you again for all your help dealing with Brewer," she added. Now caught and in Newgate, Brewer wouldn't be hurting anyone else for a long time to come.

"Our pleasure." Charles grinned and slapped Thomas on the back. "I can see why you like such an adventurous life. The danger and excitement. The altercation in the park was bloody exhilarating."

Stephen looked heavenward. "It wouldn't have been so exhilarating if you'd been shot or sliced through. You'd best stick with politics."

Charles didn't give Stephen more than a passing glance. "How soon do you set sail?" he asked Thomas.

Thomas squeezed her hand. "Later this week." Although the Ruby Cross had been retrieved from Brewer and a buyer found, Thomas's ship would take some time to obtain. And yet, he hadn't shown any disappointment at the delay. Instead, he had spoken with Gordon Lamont about a new commission, for both himself and his crew. Luckily, Mr. Lamont had heartily agreed, and they would soon be sailing on a newly acquired merchantman.

The guests formed a procession of sorts toward the location of the wedding breakfast. "We'd best follow along or we'll get nothing to eat," she suggested.

Jonas, being his usual self, had a gathering of Thomas's crew around him as he displayed his *abilities*. He stood on his head, performed his own style of dance, and elicited chuckles with his silly jokes. How he enjoyed the attention.

Thomas followed where her attention lay. "He'll certainly enliven the ship."

That he would. And from the kind looks and playful

comments from the men, they'd have plenty of help looking after him. Jonas had gone from no father at all to a whole ship full of men eager to care for him, including her captain.

She and Thomas approached the group.

"Time to eat," Thomas called out, and the crew hooted and nodded their approval. He bent low before Jonas as the men walked away. "I have something for you," he said.

"What?" Jonas's eyes widened. Her poor boy had never received much in the way of gifts.

"A wedding present." Thomas held out the pocket watch his father had given him. "For you."

Jonas's broad grin revealed the gap where he'd just lost one of his teeth. "Thank you, sir."

"My pleasure. Now let's find some food." Thomas took Jonas's hand and offered her the other. "Come along, wife."

Tenderness washed over her, and she could barely draw a breath as she grasped hold of his hand. Today was the beginning of a new life she'd never dreamed she'd have. A life full of joy with her son, and with Thomas as her husband, the love of her life.

OTHER BOOKS BY TAMARA HUGHES

Tempting the Pirate

Beauty's Curse

Once Upon a Masquerade

Author's Note

When I was thinking about the stories I wanted in the Love on the High Seas series, I couldn't resist inventing a female pirate character. Back in the day, a handful of women did dare to enter the profession. Some were wives of pirates. Others were drawn to the occupation, just like the men, for the chance at riches. Anne Bonny and Mary Read were well-known pirates in the Caribbean in the eighteenth century.

These women dressed as men in an effort to be treated like men by their brethren. In fact, Mary Read was successful in making her crew actually believe she was a man named Mark Read, at least for a time. Interestingly, she ended up on Anne Bonny's ship, and the two sailed together for a while.

These female pirates inspired the development of my character Catherine Fry, a fearless woman who had the strength to stand up to any man who stood in the way of her goals.

Thomas Glanville, on the other hand, is a character from

Tempting the Pirate, the first book in the Love on the High Seas series. In that initial book, he was first mate of the hero, James Lamont. But I liked him so much, I decided he needed his own chance at love.

The tricky part was figuring out his inner conflict. In *Tempting the Pirate*, he's a bit impulsive and, in a sense, acts against James in his effort to achieve their goal. Which tells me that he's overly ambitious and not really a team player. So why not put him in a situation where he is required to suppress his ambitions and join forces with Catherine, a woman who attacked his ship and "tortured" him.

Ha! The torture part was a hoot to write. I loved that Catherine couldn't bring herself to hurt him and had to find alternative ways to try to get him to tell her where he'd hidden the Ruby Cross. The sexual tension and the banter between the two was so much fun for me. And hopefully, for you, too.

I loved the way these two butted heads. They both were confident and headstrong, each pushing for their own agenda. It was interesting to see what it took for each of them to come to trust each other and agree to concede some control to the other in order to make their partnership work.

His Pirate Seductress was a joy to write. I love stories that can make me laugh, and this one certainly did. Thomas and Catherine really did belong together, and their journey was an adventure I reveled in. I hope you enjoyed their story as much as I did. Until next time. Happy reading!

Acknowledgments

First and foremost, I'd like to thank my critique partners and friends, Barbara Longley and Wyndemere Coffey. Your sound advice truly enrich my stories, and your encouragement keeps me going.

Thank you to Jeff, Brenna, and Megan for just being you and making me incredibly happy. To Ron and Shirley Bores, my unwavering supporters, thank you for all that you do to share my writing news and get my books into readers' hands.

And of course, thank you to my editor at Entangled Publishing, Erin Molta, for your insight and keen editing skills. My books shine because of you. Also a shout-out to the Midwest Fiction Writers. As always, you guys rock! And to the Romance Writers of America, who help guide and teach writers at all levels as they progress on this crazy journey.

Finally, a huge thank you to my readers. You wonderful, lovely people. Every review and message I receive is a blessing that makes my day. If you'd like to chat, visit me on

Twitter @TamHughes or on Facebook. Or you can contact me via my website at www.tamarahughes.com.

About the Author

A small town girl with a big imagination, Tamara Hughes had no idea what to do with her life. After graduating from college, she moved to a big city, started a family and a job, and still struggled to find that creative outlet she craved. An avid reader of romance, she gave writing a try and became hooked on the power of exploring characters, envisioning adventures, and creating worlds. She enjoys stories with interesting twists and heroines who have the grit to surmount any obstacle, all without losing the ability to laugh. To learn more, stop by her website: www.tamarahughes.com.

www.ingramcontent.com/pod-product-compliance
Lightning Source LLC
Chambersburg PA
CBHW020630180626
46816CB00003B/893